RESONANT BLUE

AND OTHER STORIES

RESO NANT BLUE

AND OTHER STORIES

TYPE EIGHTEEN
BOOKS

MARY VENSEL WHITE

Stories from this collection first appeared, in earlier forms, in the following literary journals and online publications: "What You Know" in *The Write Launch*; "Smoke" in *december magazine*; "Driftwood" *The Madison Review*; "Par Avion" in *The Write Launch*; "Griffin" in *Catapult*; and "Prism" in *The Lindenwood Review*. "Driftwood' was a finalist in *december magazine*'s Curt Johnson Prose Awards, and "Cadmium" was a finalist in the Tucson Festival of Books Literary Awards.

Library of Congress Cataloging-in-Publication Data

Names: White, Mary Vensel, 1968–, author.
Title: Resonant Blue and Other Stories / Mary Vensel White.
Description: 218 pages. – First edition. | Laguna Hills, California: Type Eighteen Books, 2025.
Summary: "The first collection of award-winning short fiction from the author of *Bellflower* and *Things to See in Arizona*. In these twelve stories, characters face turning points. Whether backed against a wall, reeling from a loss, or forced to confront a painful truth, they doggedly pursue the glimmer of possibility shining on the horizon."—Provided by publisher.
Identifiers: LCCN 2025939623 | ISBN: 9798992040579 (paperback) | ISBN: 9798992040586 (ebook)
LC record available at https://lccn.loc.gov/2025939623

Published by Type Eighteen Books
www.typeeighteenbooks.com

Printed in the United States

For Cheryle, whose porch light is always on.

TABLE OF CONTENTS

GRIFFIN

As Nora lay in bed, the scratching sound that had infiltrated her dream magnified and filled in. Scratch, scratch, scratch, like claws on newspaper. She lifted her head slightly to listen. The sun beamed through a crack in the chintz curtains, a hint of the warm California day taking shape outside. When she turned onto her side, this slice of sunshine stretched across her abdomen, cutting her body into two shadowed parts. She remembered: their daughter, Erin, was arriving that day.

Another sound filtered in, the splatter and slap of water, momentarily interrupting the scratching. When Nora was young, her stepfather bought three chickens—a rooster and two hens—and tried to teach responsibility to her and her brothers by making them care for the birds. Nora was only ten and her brothers eleven and seven, and her stepfather, although well-meaning, gave instructions that were incomplete and inconsistent. Often, they'd forget about the chickens for days at a time. When something had killed one of the hens, Nora was the one who found the bloody mess and ran inside to tell her mother. Another time, the rooster escaped and chased a neighbor's cat; her older brother was spanked for leaving the gate open. Eventually, the birds were gone, and Nora couldn't think now what had happened, when they'd died or been removed from the yard.

She stood up, walked to the window, and peered out.

Alan was shirtless, bent over the concrete slab in their backyard, pushing sudsy water around with an old, wooden broom. The bristles scratched against the cement, and his sweaty back gleamed in the morning sun.

"What in the—" Nora mumbled to herself, pulling her robe on. She drew the colorful curtains all the way back, wondering, as she always did, about her younger self. The woman who had chosen the garish pattern of vines, fat leaves, and bursting cabbage roses. The roses were coral pink and pale blue, and the vines and leaves were such a dark green they appeared almost black. All in all, colors quite unlike anything you'd find in actual nature. Nora made a mental note, as she always did, to replace the curtains. She was no longer the twenty-six-year-old Nora who'd envisioned a Laura-Ashley-themed life and yet, the buying of new curtains was something that never seemed to make headway on her many lists of things to do. Maybe she could ask Erin if she'd like to help redecorate during her visit. Erin was supposed to stay for several days, after finishing her radiology conference downtown and before heading back to Denver, where she lived. Nora and Alan hadn't seen their daughter for close to a year, but it was a contented absence. Many times throughout her life, they'd wondered if Erin would ever survive on her own for more than a few weeks or a few months, before coming back for money, for reassurance, for recovery. Still, Nora felt nervous and knew her husband's early morning activity was symptomatic of the same uncertainty.

In the kitchen, a small puddle of coffee shone next to the French press Alan used whenever he wanted his morning brew especially strong. Nora noted that the carafe was almost empty.

She wondered what time he'd woken up, if he'd slept much at all.

She pulled her shoulders back and walked outside. The patio furniture was spread out on the lawn. He had turned everything upside-down to scrape out the spiders and their webs. On the grass, the cushions were scattered like swollen, orange steppingstones.

"Careful," Alan called. "I've rinsed off the patio."

"I see that," she said.

He stood in belted khaki shorts and bare feet, the broom propped beside him.

"You look like that painting," she told him. "You know, the farmer and his pitchfork."

"American Gothic," he said. His upper lip was gleaming with sweat.

"Have you eaten?"

"I had the rest of the pasta primavera," he said.

"For breakfast?" She noted the pasty color of his face, his hunched shoulders.

"It was good," he said.

They'd gone to Vincenzo's the night before, a favorite restaurant nestled in a strip mall near their house. They'd shared a bottle of Chianti, and Alan had ordered a glass of Moscato after that. Nora had watched him carefully as he drank. He'd talked about Erin and her husband, and about how they planned to move back to California after Justin's hematology study was complete. Both he and Erin worked at the University of Colorado hospital. They'd been married for seven years, but there'd been no talk of children.

Over dinner, Alan also told Nora the long story of the vendor who'd tried to get away with partial payment on a huge shipment of semiconductors. Alan claimed to have hounded the man across oceans, threatening to board a private jet he did not own with bodyguards he did not employ in tow. Nora had heard the story many times, but last night, Alan told the funny version, not the one where he ends up indignant and furious all over again. Nora had been quite fuzzy and comfortable from the Chianti and had enjoyed the telling, all the while thinking in spurts of Erin, important and controlled in her white coat, walking the halls at the hospital in Colorado.

"What time did she say?" Alan asked now, wiping sweat from his brow.

"Maybe four o'clock." Nora left off the fact that she had given him this information a dozen times already.

He brushed the last bit of soapy water onto the lawn. "I still need to buy the short ribs."

"Is that all right for the grass?" she asked.

He looked up, one strand of wet, brown hair flipped onto his forehead. "What?"

"That soap," she said. "Will it hurt the lawn?"

"Of course it won't." He walked over and let the broom handle fall against the house, where it clanged against the window shutters. "What do you take me for?" He held his hands out; they were smeared with dirt and water. "Have you noticed at any point during our thirty-three years together, I mean, have you looked out the window to see patches of dead grass? Really, Nora, you can take over the yard work any time you'd like, instead of questioning everything I do." He leaned over and the flap of his belly covered the front of the leather belt. He lifted one of the patio chairs and pushed it loudly into position under the umbrella. His jaw clenched. "You know, I'm just trying, Nora, to make things nice for today."

"Okay, Alan, okay."

He looked at her, pushed his hair back with a clawed, rigid hand. "I'm out here working, and that's all you can say?"

Overhead, two geese honked by, refugees from the nearby

man-made lake. Their long shadows traveled the length of the yard.

She saw it clearly now, the strain in his eyes, the three deepening lines splitting his brow. "It looks great," she said.

"I can't do everything," he said. "If I was here all day—"

Her privileged life, she thought. "Would you like some more coffee?" she asked. "Maybe iced?" She wanted to add, "Wouldn't plain water work just fine?" Or, "Calm down." Any number of reasonable things people say. Slowly, she edged towards the door.

"Sure," he said. "I hardly slept."

When she looked back, he was concentrating again on the task, hauling the patio furniture back onto the cement, patting the cushions into place.

Erin was an adorable baby. Curly blonde hair, creamy skin, and a radiant smile. That is not to say her older brother, Kyle, hadn't been cute in his own way. Brown wavy hair, crooked smile, those meaty little hands. He was a handsome man now, completely respectable and always kind-hearted. But Erin had charmed everyone she'd ever met, especially her father.

Nora put on the kettle and cleaned out the French press. She wasn't a coffee drinker herself, and the process always seemed unnecessarily messy. Teabags were much more sensible, each its own easily disposable container. She'd grown to hate the smell of coffee.

Alan appeared in the door frame. "I'm going to shower." He looked at some point over her head. "I still need to buy the short ribs and wash the car."

"She won't notice the car," Nora said.

"Needs done anyway." He rummaged through the kitchen junk drawer and then shut it loudly. "It's ten o'clock already." He stood looking at her expectantly.

"Don't worry," she said, cautiously.

"I'm not," he said. "I promise, I'm not. I'll shower first." He walked by and gave her waist a quick squeeze.

Nora leaned against the counter, taking deep breaths, until she heard the steady stream of water upstairs. Then she dumped the contents of the French press into the sink.

———

"THIS TRAFFIC!" Erin breezed into the living room, a leather duffel hanging from one shoulder and a red, rectangular purse clutched against her chest. Her blonde hair, no longer curly, was pulled back into a ponytail. "I'd forgotten how bad it can be."

Alan leaned over and hugged her awkwardly, around the purse. "Pretty congested where you are too, Dove. Took forty minutes from the airport last time."

She maneuvered around him and pressed her face against Nora's. She smelled like rain, talcum powder, and vaguely, something sour. Nora held her for a moment too long, and they both backed up, chuckling.

"Really, Dad, there's no comparison." Erin opened her purse, found a case for her sunglasses, and snapped them inside. "The walkway looks good," she said to Nora.

They'd had it done, whitewashed pavers with a thin, stone trim. Alan's pet project because Nora had thought the old red bricks looked fine. "Your father picked everything," she said.

"Nice." She walked past them, down the hall to her old room.

Alan fidgeted. "Should I start the barbecue then?"

"Not yet," Nora said. "Let her settle in."

Erin reappeared at the opening to the hallway. "You got a new bedspread for my bed. Very chic."

Nora couldn't tell if her daughter was pleased or not. "The old one was frayed," she explained.

They wandered out to the backyard, but Erin declared it too warm, so they sat at the kitchen table instead. Nora poured sun tea for everyone, and Erin put two large spoonfuls of sugar into hers, as she had done since she was a teenager. They watched her stir and stir until the granules dissolved.

"Everything all right with Justin?" Alan asked.

Erin's eyes narrowed. "What do you mean?"

"The study, his work. Still looking to finish this winter?"

Nora noted her daughter's pink silk shirt, the tailored herringbone skirt. A smudge of eye shadow had made its way onto her temple, and the ponytail was crooked. Erin had probably pulled her hair back in the car, because of the heat. She had probably been much more put-together for her conference. "Don't you want to change into something comfortable?" Nora asked.

Erin shook her head and looked at her father. "Yeah, the study should be finished in November, but it looks like he'll be offered a permanent position."

Alan leaned forward, his hands folded. "Oh. I didn't—I mean, we didn't know that was a possibility." A vein in his temple pulsed.

"We're happy about it."

"That's wonderful," Nora said.

"Justin really likes his colleagues," she said.

"And you're still happy with your job?" Nora asked.

Erin shrugged. "It could be worse. The people are nice, but I'm getting the worst hours, and the place is so busy all the time."

"It's a hospital," Alan said. His glass clanked against his teeth as he took a drink of iced tea.

Nora got up to get the snack she had prepared. "Can you ask for another shift?" she asked.

"I have to wait until one of the senior people leave, or someone above me wants to change."

"Seniority," Alan said. "All jobs work that way. You keep your head down, put in the time. Eventually, there are benefits. Everywhere you go, there are short timers. The world needs them, I guess, but they're not the ones who get ahead. Quitting never got anyone ahead."

Erin shook her head, looked at her mother. "Who said anyone was quitting?"

Nora set a plate of crackers and cheese on the table and put her hand on Alan's shoulder. She felt the sinew and bone, the quivering muscle underneath.

Upstairs, a thump sounded against one of the windows. "What was that?" Nora asked.

"I didn't hear anything," Erin said.

Nora stood up. "Do you need to rest for a while? Your father got the short ribs you like."

"I haven't been eating much meat lately," their daughter said.

"There's salad, too," Nora told her.

Alan slurped his tea and then got up and noisily put his glass into the sink.

"Maybe I will go and change clothes," Erin said. "I've been wearing this since five this morning."

"There are clean towels if you want to shower," Nora said, glancing over at Alan. "Take your time. We're so glad you're here."

Nora and Erin watched as he opened the refrigerator and closed it, then opened the drawer next to the sink, then closed that.

"Alan?" Nora said, but he hadn't heard her. Lips moving, he left the kitchen.

———

NORA WAS TOSSING the salad for dinner when a shadow passed over the counter. A flutter of air lifted the hair from her neck, and she shivered. She looked over her shoulder at the high corner, where an antique milk jug filled with fake plants sat on top of the cupboard. "I know you're back there," she whispered. She hadn't seen Alan for a while, but she'd heard him in the back yard, knocking things around in the shed at the side of the house. She'd smelled the gas when he started the barbecue.

"Can I help?" Erin asked. Her hair was wet, and she'd changed into yoga pants and a long tee shirt with Telluride in big, block letters.

Nora finished putting plastic wrap over the top of the salad bowl and wrapped her arms around her daughter's waist, pulling her close. "Oh, I missed you."

Erin exhaled, let herself be hugged. "Where's Dad?"

"Cooking the ribs. Can't you have a little?"

"I'm an A positive blood type," she said. "We don't do well with meat. Have you heard about the blood type diet?"

Nora released her, shook her head. "I'm A positive, too," she said. "You must have gotten that from me."

"Maybe you should skip the meat then."

The back door opened, and Alan came in. "There they are," he said, "my two little ladies."

"It's weird when you say it like that," Erin said. "What are we drinking, Mom?"

Nora found the bottle of Cabernet they'd purchased. Just one bottle.

Erin took the wine from Nora and went to the drawer for an opener. "What's new at your job, Dad?"

"Ah, you know the import-export business, Dove."

"Lots of comings and goings," she said.

It was something he always said, thinking it was funny.

Erin poured three glasses and handed them around. "Salut."

Nora kept herself busy at the stove, stirring potatoes that were already mashed, checking on the green beans with the tiny slivers of almonds that Erin liked. She took a sip of wine, unsure whether she should drink her share or keep her wits.

One of the worst times she'd ever had was Erin's accident. That day, and the night that followed, and the haze of days afterward. Nora drove back and forth between home and the hospital, where Erin lay with a broken collarbone, three broken fingers, and a perforated left lung. One scorching afternoon during this distressing time, Nora found Alan in the garage, perched in the storage loft with his father's Army pistol from the Korean War. Kyle had just left for college, thank God, and Nora's stepfather came over to talk his son-in-law down. Nora was ashamed and didn't know what to say. Over the years, she'd been able to handle Alan, to contain everything, but after seeing Erin in the hospital, he'd unraveled like never before. Nora called Dr. Harrison for a sedative, which her stepfather kindly picked up. She fixed dinner for both men, coaxed her stepfather into his car, and waited for Alan to sleep. Then she drove back to see Erin.

Even now, these many years later, Nora's heart skipped a beat when she remembered the phone call from the police. Erin had driven her car into a cement barrier at the aqueduct. She'd been drinking with friends after a school dance. She was seventeen, continually at odds with her dad, who had always held her too close, and she was prone to excessive behaviors. Yes, in Nora's estimation, that was one of the very worst times, Erin pale and damaged, and the maelstrom at home. For those long, sleepless days, Nora never knew what to expect from either of them. She found strength in remembering those horrible days; everything that came after didn't compare and so, she always knew she could get through whatever setback came.

Erin nibbled on her salad during dinner, picking out the

mushrooms she used to like, using only a dab of dressing. Nora thought their daughter looked rather thin and wasn't sure how she hadn't noticed before.

Alan held a short rib in his greasy fingers. The sauce had found its way to his chin, and the collar of the golf shirt he'd worn for dinner. "You're missing out, Dove. How long have you been a vegan?"

"I'm not a vegan, Dad, or even a vegetarian. I haven't been eating much meat, that's all."

He leaned across the table, reaching for the wine. "What does Justin think about that?"

Erin's eyebrows were creased. "What does he think about what?"

"Your diet." Alan looked at Nora and shrugged.

"I haven't asked him. See, we have a lot of freedom in our marriage, to live our own lives."

Nora closed her eyes.

"What?" He looked back and forth between them.

Erin got up and went to the kitchen. She came back with another bottle of wine that Nora had hidden on a shelf with the canned food.

"I'm not sure we need to open that," Nora said.

Erin's mouth spread into a sly smile. "Dad will help me with this, won't you?"

He waved his hand. "Open it."

Once Erin was home and healing after the accident, Nora's stepfather had called one evening. He wanted to know what in God's green earth was going on with Alan, whether it was something Nora had to deal with regularly, whether she needed any help. He and Nora's mother had recently suffered the first health setback of their own, a minor heart attack that had landed him in the hospital. He'd always known that Alan was moody, he said, but this seemed like something else. Nora reassured him, and reassured herself that she could manage it.

———

LATER, they were in the backyard, sitting on the cushions that still felt damp to Nora; she knew better than to mention it. In the trees, on the roof; the scratch of claws, the musical chirps.

"That is not what happened!" Alan said. "I was always supportive of the gymnastics. I didn't understand why you kept starting and stopping, then starting again."

"What did it matter?" Erin leaned her head against the seat-back, her wineglass held to her chest with both hands. "I was a kid. I changed my mind."

"It matters!" Alan said. "When you join something, you commit. All in, or why bother?"

"It's not the Army," she cackled. "We're talking about gymnastics classes for a ten-year-old."

"Your mother was too easy on you and your brother. I would have insisted you stick with it, at least for a couple of years. You have to give everything time."

"What do you mean, you would have done this or that? You lived here at the time, you know!" Erin raised the glass to her lips, and the red liquid looked black and thick in the muted light.

Alan spread his legs, sitting up in his chair. "Dedication to the thing, that's what's required. My first job was at the hardware store and—do you know—I worked there every summer for four years."

"And the owner made you count nails and screws, and you didn't think it was really something that needed to be done but you did it, anyway, because you had commitment and dedication." Erin recited this in a sing-song voice.

"You've done well with this new job?" Alan asked.

"Would you believe me if I said I have?"

In the corner of the yard sat an old Magnolia tree. Nora heard a rustle, something scampering from branch to branch. She looked across the grass, watching for movement amidst the dark leaves. I'm losing my mind, she thought.

"Nora," Alan said. "Tell our daughter she's done well."

"She knows what I think," she said.

Erin finished her wine and reached for the second bottle, which was propped on an empty chair and was almost empty, too.

Alan held his glass out.

Two Christmases ago, Kyle had brought his wife and newborn daughter for the holiday. Nora had prepared his old room, bought food and presents, scrubbed and arranged. The last thing he'd said before they left for the hotel was, "I don't know how you do it, Mom. Or why."

"Have I ever done anything right?" Erin asked. "No, really, try to be objective. Name one thing I've ever done you thought was okay. Start to finish. Good decision, good implementation, great result. Anything?"

"Erin," Nora said.

Alan looked down at his hands, brow furrowed. "Well, of course, there are so many things. Look at you now, Dove."

"I'm tired," Erin said. "Such a long day."

"Can we talk about this?" Alan said to Nora.

"I'm tired, too," she said.

His eyes were black and blazing. "You're crazy if you think I'll allow the two of you to turn against me."

"What did I do?" Nora asked.

"This is always how it goes, right? The two of you, against me. Good thing Kyle's not here, or I'd really be outnumbered."

Nora sighed, stuck in her chair. "No one's against anyone."

Erin drank her wine, looking back and forth between them.

Nora remembered now: one surviving hen and the rooster had escaped. One day they were there, and the next they weren't. No one in her family ever talked about this, their collective guilt. Once, when traveling along the dirt roads near the house, Nora saw the rooster—or at least she thought it was *their* rooster—walking alongside an empty lot, stopping now and then to peck at the ground. And she felt a strange mixture of relief and culpability and unsettledness. Was the rooster happy to be away from their yard, where food and attention were unreliable? Or was he truly lost, wishing for the tiny wooden house, feathers littered all around, and the shady pen he could fly over any time? Basically, was his life better or worse as a result of this freedom? That's what she wondered, and she could never figure it out.

"You have always interfered with my relationships with the kids," Alan said. "It has ruined everything."

"I don't know what you mean."

"If you had any idea what I have to go through during the day," he said.

"Alan, I'm tired. Erin's tired. You were both up early this morning."

He threw his wine glass against the side of the house, where it shattered and left a dripping, red stain.

"The neighbors!" Nora said. "What is wrong with you?"

And so it went, angry whispers and pleading and accusations and recriminations. The night air swirled around Alan's head, lifting his thinning hair in tufts. Dozens of glinting eyes peered out from the trees. Something was scratching on the roof. Nora covered her ears, covered her eyes, watched everything and saw nothing.

"Let's stop," she finally said, but this only made him more furious.

ALAN ROSE UP from his patio chair and shook off his golf shirt, which fell in tatters onto the cement. Above him, the outdoor lights glowed yellow on his bare skin. Next to Nora, Erin pulled her knees to her chest and buried her face. Nora threw one arm across their daughter, a barrier, a blockade. Against the night sky, in the jaundice gleam of the canned lights, Alan hovered above them. A great whoosh, the extinguishing of light and noise, and two large, black wings extended from his body. They were great to behold, majestic and strong, and they stretched to a great height and extended to a great breadth. They blocked everything out. When he began to beat them, to unfurl the terrible expanse of feathers and darkness, the gust of air forced the remaining wine glasses from the table, blew the back door shut and spurred Erin to seek shelter in her childhood room. Nora imagined her there, underneath the stylish bedspread, fuming and remembering, fuming and remembering. Eventually, wings were tucked in for the night; black eyes closed amongst the branches.

NORA WOKE early and started the coffee. Both women would need it, that much was certain. She looked through the kitchen window. Another perfect, sunny day. The yard showed no evidence of the squall the night before. She had stayed up until the house was orderly and quiet.

Erin came into the kitchen, fully dressed in a pair of jeans and a white button-up shirt. The red purse hung from her shoulder; she set the duffel on the tile floor.

"Coffee?" Nora asked.

"Thanks."

She sat down at the table, cupped her hands around the mug.

"Do you want toast? Eggs?"

"No thanks."

Nora sat across from Erin. "Have you finished fixing up the new apartment?"

"Hm? Yes, we're all unpacked. I had to buy a few things but not much."

"I'd love to come see it."

"You should! Why couldn't you, Mom? We'd love to have you."

Nora set her cup down. "Maybe I will."

Erin looked well-rested, calm. She'd pulled her hair back again, only this time, the ponytail was neat and curled a bit at the ends. "I changed my flight," she said.

"Will Justin pick you up?"

"Yes."

"And things are okay?"

Erin shrugged. "We're having a rough patch, but we'll get through."

"Yes, you will." Nora reached over and squeezed her hand. "I've been volunteering down at the senior center where I take Grandma."

"Really?"

"I help plan some of the social activities, organize bridge tournaments or movie nights, stuff like that. They've asked me to take a paying position."

"Makes sense," Erin said.

"What?"

"You, taking care of people."

"They are so appreciative, so happy to have someone there."

"That's great, Mom." Erin stood and put her mug on the

counter. "I have to go." She exhaled, her shoulders shaking a bit at the end. "I really hate flying."

"I know you do," Nora said. She got up and hugged her daughter, took in the smell and feel of her, trying her hardest to store the sensations.

Erin picked up her duffle, and they walked to the door. Outside, the sun was relentless.

At the end of the walkway, Erin turned, opened her mouth.

"Don't," Nora said.

Overhead, a formation passed by, merely blips against the big, blue sky, tiny, insignificant forms from that distance, organized and close knit and moving forward with some inherent, uncommunicated purpose.

Nora watched Erin load her things into the rental car and drive away. She looked down the quiet street at the line of similar houses, then she walked down the new, stone path and went inside.

PRISM

"Look what I did."

Her mother stands at the window, one hand holding back the pale green curtain, the other propped on her hip. She is wearing the long nightgown again.

Shane rubs the sleep from her eyes and walks toward her. Leaning forward, she peers out. The lawn shines from the morning sprinklers, and the sky is the bluest blue.

"I did that," her mother says, watching the driveway.

Behind the car, the air is wavy with exhaust. Shane catches a glimpse of Brian's white coat, hanging from a wire hanger in the backseat, before the car speeds away.

She turns and presses her face into her mother's side. The yelling woke her from a dream she's now remembering, something about saving a baby pig, something about a farm. The yelling, the slam of the front door, and the crash of the framed photograph that fell from the wall.

"Is he coming back?" she asks.

Her mother lets the curtain drop. "I don't know." She pulls Shane into the firm, round expanse of her belly. "You must be hungry," she says.

In the foyer, the picture has shattered into several large shards. Her mother isn't wearing any shoes, so Shane says she'll clean it up. She finds the broom and dustpan in the garage, and her mother's flip flops in the shoe organizer Brian bought and spent a Saturday afternoon assembling. There's also a bookshelf in the living room and a bench for the dining table she and her mother brought from their apartment. Brian grunted up the steps with each unwieldy box and propped them against the wall. He asked Shane to help put the furniture together, but she cut paper liners for the kitchen cupboards instead.

"Be careful," her mother calls out. "Scrambled or sunny side up?"

"Scrambled, please."

The photograph is one they took at the pier in Santa Monica. They stood in front of the Ferris wheel with its yellow and red carriages and her mother asked a lady to take it for them. Shane is smaller, reaching only her mother's hip. They're both wearing big plastic sunglasses like movie stars. Carefully, Shane shakes the glass fragments off the image and into the dustpan. She remembers that day. She won a stuffed caterpillar, and they shared a double scoop of mint chocolate. That was two summers ago, before Brian.

A bad smell is coming from the kitchen. Shane puts the frame on the bookshelf and takes the dustpan with her. At the stove, her mother is looking out the window at the brick wall while the eggs burn.

"Mom," Shane says.

Her mother's face is wet with tears.

Shane reaches around her and shuts off the burner. "Let me do it," she says.

The bench squeaks across the floor as her mother sits down.

"Do you want some tea, the orange kind?"

"I would love that."

Shane fills a mug with water from the tap and puts it in the microwave to heat. She scrapes the eggs from the skillet, cleans it, and sets it back on the stove. On her tiptoes, she reaches the box of teabags in the cupboard.

"My big girl," her mother says.

"Do you want eggs too?"

"I had oatmeal," she says.

Shane looks at her mother, who has moved from the bench to one of the chairs. Her feet, puffy and white, are splayed in a wide v. "Oatmeal again?"

"It's the only thing I want to eat lately." She rests her hands on the shelf of her abdomen.

"Is she kicking?" Shane asks.

"No," her mother says. "But she's getting bigger, taking up all the room."

Shane brings the tea to her mother, with the pink and white box of sugar and a spoon. "Did I do that?"

She smiles. "All in all, you were a much more considerate tenant."

"What's tenant?"

"Someone who's staying, just for a while."

Shane thinks *like Brian* but doesn't say it. She remembers their apartment on the second floor, the leaves swishing against her window and the neighbor's yellow cat sunning himself on the stairs outside. Before that, the small house with the shady porch. Her father's motorcycle propped in the driveway.

"I'm going to get dressed," her mother says. "When you finish your breakfast, we'll go out for a while."

"Where?"

"Errands, maybe lunch." She gets up slowly from the chair. The nightdress stays bunched up under her breasts. Two dark outlines show through the thin fabric.

Shane wonders if they'll be able to stay in the new house

without Brian. She can easily imagine it; almost everything is theirs. He brought a few things from his place—a big TV, the brown couch, a piano—but the rest is in a storage unit. She'd heard them talk about cleaning it out, some weekend after the baby is born. Maybe he can get his apartment back, Shane thinks. It might still be empty.

They've been in the new house for two months. Her mother had to drive her the last few weeks of school. Shane doesn't mind starting a new school for fourth grade. At her old school, she hadn't had any playdates for a long time and during lunch, Mrs. Smith let her stay in the classroom if she wanted. Shane had worked her way through the entire third grade library. Mrs. Smith had a special note from the school counselor, the same note Miss Lingard had the year before.

The new house would be perfect for three. The crib was already set up next to her mother's bed and when the baby got bigger, Shane would share her room. They could still have adventures and sleep on a pile of blankets in the living room if they wanted.

Her mother comes out in a striped tee shirt and denim shorts. The shorts have a stretchy section in the front, but it's hidden under the shirt. Some lipstick is smeared on her teeth and her eyes are wet again.

"We can stay home," Shane says. She is wearing a tie-dyed dress she loves. She's been wearing it all week.

Her mother grabs the keys from one of the hooks Brian hung by the front door.

"We're not going to the store, are we?" Shane asks.

"Come on," she says.

Her mother works at the checkout at CVS, but she's having her maternity time now. Brian is one of the pharmacists. He works in the back, but it didn't stop him from meeting her mother. The first time he came to their apartment, they had dinner and watched a movie. Shane told her mother afterwards he had big teeth and talked funny, and her mother sent her to bed.

Outside, the sun peeks through the trees. Shane squints and sees the red, dented car, which her mother insists on parking in the street because Brian's car is nicer. Shane opens the passenger door only a little, so she won't scrape it on the curb.

Her mother's hands are shaking a little when she puts the key in the ignition. Her belly leaves only a few inches of space between her and the steering wheel. "Seatbelt," she says.

Shane reaches over to get it, biting her lip. Sometimes she doesn't think about her father for a long time. Sometimes, a simple thing brings it all back: the hospital, the twisted motorcycle, her mother lying on the kitchen floor, kicking.

Her mother reaches over and flips on the air conditioner. She hasn't turned on the radio, but Shane won't ask.

"Do you remember when we had the singing contest?" Shane says. "You did that old song, what was it called?"

"Time After Time."

"And Daddy sang the one about the bridge and did all the dance moves." She watches her mother.

"I remember."

"You got me that microphone for my birthday."

"We did."

"Where is it now?"

Her mother stops at a light, looks at Shane, shrugs.

They drive for a while in silence. Shane sees a woman with three children walking down the street. A black truck drives by, windows down and music loud. Her mother turns onto a familiar street.

"I thought you said we weren't going to the store," Shane says.

Her mother looks at her quickly, as though she's surprised to find her in the car. "You don't understand," she says. "I have to see." Quickly, she pulls into a parking space in the corner of the CVS lot.

"Understand what?" Shane asks. "See what?"

Her mother shakes her head, slowly at first then faster. She covers her face with her hands, and her fingers make creases in her forehead.

"Okay, Mom, stop." Tentatively, Shane touches her arm.

She pulls Shane's hand against her chest as her eyes focus on the rearview mirror.

They wait in the car for two hours until Brian finally comes out. Shane knows when he appears because she senses the change in the air, a tensing of her mother's body. She had been almost asleep, thinking again about the baby pig, alone in a crate. She realizes now that the farm is the same one where they picked strawberries one time. Her mother wore a bandanna over her curly hair, and her father napped in the car. They'd been arguing on the drive over, and he'd refused to get out. There weren't any animals at the real place, only a locked barn and a shed to get the buckets for picking.

Her mother exhales, a sound like air going out of a balloon.

Shane turns in her seat and watches as Brian and a woman walk toward them. She is tall and thin, with black hair and long, silver earrings that flash in the sunlight. They're carrying several plastic bags, which they put into Brian's car before they get in and drive off.

Her mother follows from a distance and a few times, Shane thinks they've lost the car. They watch as Brian parks at an apartment building, and he and the woman get the bags out of the car. The woman gives some of her bags to Brian so she can punch in the code at the front gate. While they are inside, Shane can hear her mother breathing in quick spurts. Brian comes out, again with the woman. They get back in his car and her mother follows. Soon, Brian parks in the CVS parking lot, and he and the woman go back inside.

Her mother turns off the car, leans her head back, and closes her eyes.

"Mom," Shane says.

"Hm?"

"Are we going to have lunch?"

She opens her eyes. "What do you think of that?"

"What?"

"Brian."

Shane remembers the yelling from the morning. "I think," she says cautiously, "he's helping her with groceries because her car is broken?"

Her mother nods. Her hair is damp at the roots, darker in color than the rest, which is a golden blonde. She pats Shane's knee, just above a fresh scrape, then pulls her over. "I'm sorry," she says.

Shane mumbles into her mother's chest. "We don't need him."

"Yes, we do." Her mother releases her. She flips down the mirror over the driver's seat, wipes mascara and tears from the corners of her eyes, and flips it back up.

Shane thinks about her grandmother, who came to stay when her mother was having a hard time. She walked Shane to school every morning and was waiting every afternoon when she came out. Her grandmother doesn't look like anyone else's. She has curly hair, too, only brown, and she wears jeans and leather boots up to her knees. She has a tattoo of a bird on her left shoulder. Her grandmother stayed with them for a long time, until her mother could take care of Shane again, until she could find a job and stay out of bed all weekend.

Shane considers calling her grandmother if Brian doesn't come back. She could help them for a little while, with the baby especially, and go back to her house in Pasadena afterwards. Once she heard her grandmother apologizing for Shane's father, who was her son. All the trouble when he was here, she said, and now this.

They buy hamburgers at a drive-thru and eat them back at the house. In the late afternoon, her mother takes a nap. Shane goes into the bedroom and covers the mound of her belly with a blanket. She lingers at the baby's crib and touches the quilt folded over the side rail. The quilt is blue and yellow, mostly with pictures of nursery rhymes. A cow jumping over the moon, five yellow ducks, a knife and a spoon.

When Shane wakes up, the house has gone gray and hazy. She is lying on the floor next to her mother's bed, covered with the baby quilt. Her feet stick out from the bottom; her hair is matted and damp. From the tunnel of the hallway, she hears a familiar sound, the clink-clink of glass. Her eyes focus on the carpet, a beige world of tiny mountains and valleys. In her fuzzy, half-awake state, she thinks it's her father making the clink-clink sounds and hopes he is his best self, the one he promised to be after the first accident, the time he broke the window and had stitches. Shane hopes her mother will sleep through whatever it is, and she can get him to bed quietly.

Folding back the quilt, she stands. On the bed, her mother is lying on her side, her blonde curls spread around her head like a halo. Shane tiptoes out of the room, follows the soft light to the kitchen.

Brian stands next to the dishwasher, unloading. He started on the top, with the glasses and bowls, even though her mother liked to do the silverware first. His blue shirt is stuck to the middle of his back with sweat.

Shane stands in the doorway and waits. A tide is rising in her, frothy and dark. She crosses her arms over her chest.

He works quickly, never pausing, and when he lifts the plastic cage of silverware and turns, he sees Shane. "Well, hello."

She is thirsty but will not ask him.

"Is she okay?" he asks. "And how are you?" He opens a drawer and starts to put away the knives, the forks, the spoons. "It's not like you to sleep in the afternoon."

Shane watches the shifting of his shoulders under the shirt. His arms are skinny and long. Her father would flex his muscles until she couldn't get her hands all the way around. She doesn't know where his weights have gone; he kept them in the garage at their house.

Brian closes the dishwasher and turns around. "Come here," he says. "I have something to show you."

She stays where she is. "What?"

"Something from the store," he says, lifting his eyebrows. "A present."

"We saw you there," she says.

He is holding a small bag. "Where?"

"At the store." Now, brazenly, she walks to the cupboard, fills a glass with water.

Brian sits on one of the two chairs from their old apartment. Shane wishes he'd sit on his stupid bench instead.

"Why didn't you say hello?" he asks.

She looks at him while she takes a long drink.

"Listen, Shane," he says. "Everything is fine, I promise you that. It's hard, carrying a baby. Your mom is worn out, that's all."

"But the last time—" She turns away.

"No," he says. "You don't have to worry."

"I'm not worried," she says.

"Okay, you're not worried. That's good." He holds the bag up, shakes it slightly. "Don't you want to see?"

She lifts one shoulder as she presses the cool rim of the glass against her lips.

He reaches in and pulls out something attached to a small string. It is circular but flat, and it twirls around.

"Is it glass?" she asks.

"Yes, but watch."

In the light from the ceiling, colors shift and spark and she sees a pattern in the glass, tiny triangles like a cut diamond.

"What do you do with it?" she asks, coming closer.

Hanging from his hand, it rotates and flashes color.

"You can hang it in your window," he says.

Shane feels the weight, the coolness, against the palm of her hand. He has been around for more than a year, she realizes. From time to time, he brings her something from the store: an umbrella-shaped nightlight, sunflower seeds, a tube of Chapstick. He cooks dinner sometimes and rubs her mother's feet. He asks Shane about school, about other things. He sometimes yells back at her mother but mostly, he doesn't.

He leans toward her, and she can smell the pharmacy on him, the stuffy air, the tang of medicine. "I'm going to stay and take care of your mom, Shane. I love her, and I love you. Do you understand?"

She steps back, looks at the floor.

"I'd better wake her, or she'll be up all night." He puts his hands on the table and pushes himself up. His white coat is folded across the back of the other chair. She sees the plastic nametag pinned above the pocket. Her mother has a similar one. She had to get a new one made after they got married. Her grandmother came that day, but her other grandparents live too far away for short notice, her mother said.

Brian walks toward the doorway, and the dark thing rushes and swells in Shane. As she rolls the string between her thumb and forefinger, the glass flickers—blue and purple and green and orange and yellow—and sends shapes of color onto the kitchen walls. She thinks about standing in that courtroom, watching her mother and Brian hold hands, and her grand-mother next to them, wiping her eyes with a crumpled tissue. She remembers another day, her father's eyes squeezed shut as he pushes his fist through the window.

Shane lifts her arm, up, up, behind her head, and throws with all her might. The gift hits the wall next to Brian's shoulder, leaving a satisfying dent in the plaster. He ducks, too late, and stumbles. It bounces loudly from the edge of the countertop, skitters across the tile floor, spinning and spinning, reflecting pulses of colored light all around, and finally comes to rest near her bare feet, still attached to the thin, white string and by all appearances, unbroken.

CADMIUM

THE CEREMONY WAS HELD in his mother's backyard. She'd rented a metal arch, which was stuck in the grass and decorated with a long strip of gauzy material and fake flowers in white and yellow. There were white folding chairs and flower petals strewn onto the grass between the chairs. Tate had stepped on these as he had walked his mother down the aisle, thinking all along how he would have sprung for real flowers on that arch, if it were him.

It was only March but already hot as hell, as it always was at his mother's place in Arizona. After the brief ceremony, everyone had scurried inside, where the air conditioning was set at a temperature that would keep meat from spoiling. Tate stood on the shaded back patio, smoking.

He'd arrived only the night before, took an evening flight from O'Hare to Phoenix and drove the twenty miles to Mesa in a rental car. His sister, Lisa, had offered to get him from the airport in her rental, but he preferred to have his own transportation, just in case. Lisa and his other sister, Estelle, had flown out together earlier in the week to help with planning. Estelle was the oldest. She'd been divorced from her husband for many years; their two boys, Greg and David, were in graduate school and college, respectively, and unable to come out for the some-what-last-minute celebration. Lisa's children were younger: Dax, 9, Luna, 7, and Stella, 2. Her husband, Jim, had stayed home with the kids. They planned to bring the whole family out in the summer, when they could stay at a local resort that had a water-park and places for the children to run and exhaust themselves. Estelle and Lisa still lived in St. Charles, where they had all grown up, but Tate had moved the forty miles into Chicago for college and had never left. He was the baby of the family, Lisa's junior by four years and Estelle's by seven. So for this weekend, it was the three of them, the original kids, without the distrac-tion of their newer families and significant others. This made Tate somewhat nervous.

Myles hadn't been happy about being excluded. Those were his words: *You're excluding me*. But Tate had insisted it wasn't a big deal. His sisters were coming without spouses and the whole thing had been thrown together, and didn't Myles have a big project at work anyway? *But I've met your mother already*, Myles had said, which was true. They had stopped during a road trip to San Diego two summers earlier. Of course, they had stayed at a hotel, and that was before Tate knew anything about his moth-er's paramour, this George Hernandez she'd married an hour ago. Isn't it Jorge, he'd asked Estelle on the phone, and she'd replied, deadpan: No, just George.

Tate stepped onto the lawn and stubbed his cigarette in the short grass. In the bright, desert sunlight, all that white—the arch, the chairs, the lattice enclosing a line of shrubbery—all of it hurt his eyes. The yard was meager, orderly, and so much smaller than what they'd had in St. Charles. He couldn't under-stand what his mother saw in the place, how she ended up in the desert.

When he went back into the house, a wall of icy air hit him.

Next to the couch—the *davenport*, his mother would say—three elderly women stood in a close circle, clutching coffee mugs.

"For as long as I live, I'll remember that red dress." The tallest of the three had curled, stiff hair that didn't move at all. "It was like something from a movie, wasn't it?" She lowered her voice. "The actor would say: 'When you die, I'll come to your funeral in a red dress, you asshole.'"

Tate's eyebrows rose involuntarily. The colorful language was surprising coming from this trio, who in their matching ensembles looked ready for a day of church, or bridge, or whatever the elderly did around the sleepy town.

The shortest one, whose arm clanked with bracelets as she pointed, said: "It fit her like a dream, too. Hugged her in all the right places. Fire engine red, that's what it was."

"He deserved it," the tall one said. "Were her shoes red too?"

The third, curvier than the other two, nodded.

"I'd call it a true red," the tall woman went on. "Crimson, maybe."

Bracelets jangled. "No, crimson is darker, like blood. Maybe candy apple, something like that."

"Cadmium," the quiet, curvy one said.

"What?"

"That's the color. Cadmium."

The other two women raised their eyebrows and indulgently, nodded. As if they were accustomed to strange pronouncements from their friend.

The tall one took a sip of her coffee. "She had nerve. I think we all saw that."

Tate wondered who they were talking about, if the woman with nerve was present, or even alive anymore. None of the calm faces around the room seemed capable of such a bold act. He turned, walked into the kitchen, and for a moment, thought he saw his mother at the counter, arranging food on a tray. But it was Estelle, wearing one of their mother's aprons. The girls had planned an assortment of appetizers—canapes, their mother would say—for the interim between the ceremony and a full, catered dinner. There were about twenty people at the wedding. They'd eat at tables outside, and hopefully, it would be cooler by then.

As Estelle moved easily around the kitchen, he wondered how often she'd been there. He opened the refrigerator and pulled out an open bottle of Pinot Grigio. "Glasses?" he asked, and Estelle pointed to a cupboard near the sink, which was where he would have checked first. Maybe there's a method to how a family places things in a kitchen. Maybe that's why Estelle knew where everything was.

"Want to try one?" She handed him a tiny piece of toasted bread, topped with cheese and some thin-sliced, pinkish meat.

"Ham?" he asked.

"Salmon."

He shoved the whole thing into his mouth and poured himself a good-sized glass of wine.

"Take it easy," Estelle said, narrowing her eyes.

"Yes, Mom."

They'd been surprised when their parents announced the move to Arizona. His father had retired from the police force late, at sixty, and although they'd silently wondered what he'd do with himself and how the two would manage all day in the house together, they never imagined something like that. At the time, Estelle's boys were young, busy with sports and activities, and she was especially hurt by their decision. Lisa was newly married but didn't have children to consider yet, and Tate had been living in the city for some time.

That was ten years ago; it had been six since their father died. They thought their mother would return to St. Charles then, and they'd been disappointed, again, when she had stayed in Mesa—the girls were disappointed, anyway. Tate didn't think about it much.

Estelle reached over, grabbed his wineglass, and took a drink.

"Get your own," he said.

She puckered her lips at him. She wore glasses now, which was a shame because she'd always had the best, brightest blue eyes. He noticed a few gray hairs near her temple, missed by the hairdresser.

"How's your job going?" he asked.

Estelle worked at the Pheasant Run Resort, a sprawling complex in St. Charles with a convention center, golf course, restaurants, and spa. She managed a little gift shop.

"Getting into the busy season," she said. "God, how I dread summer sometimes. Looking forward to having the boys home, though."

"How are they?"

She nodded. "Good, good. One more year in the MBA program for Greg, two more at Urbana-Champaign for David. No idea what he'll do after that."

"What's his major lately?"

"History."

Tate reached around her and grabbed another appetizer, and she tried, too late, to swat him away.

Estelle was tall and slim like their mother. He was the only one to inherit their father's stockier build, which was probably for the best, him being the only male. Their mother didn't often wear heels, because their father had never liked her being taller than him.

"What about you?" she asked. "Work, I mean."

Tate worked in the accounting department of a marketing firm. "Still crunching numbers," he said.

"And how's Myles?"

"Very well."

She leaned over the counter and lowered her voice. "Why didn't he come?"

"You know why."

Estelle frowned. "She's different."

"People don't change," he said.

She shook her head and continued arranging the canapes on a silver tray. "Did you see how nervous she was? I've never seen her like that, not once. She's always been the epitome of control." She paused to look at him. "My whole childhood, I never thought of her as a *person*, because she was always there to support me, to help me with whatever *I* wanted to do. Did you feel that way?"

He shrugged.

"Of course, I was thinking about Daddy and feeling strange about the whole thing, maybe even disloyal. But I can't help being happy for her. She's never done anything for herself, not really."

"What about moving here?"

"That was for Daddy."

"Okay," he said.

She straightened up. "You're the one who won't change."

"What are you talking about?"

"It was a long time ago," she said.

"So was your divorce, but you're still pissed about that."

Her face flashed anger, but she recovered. "Not the same." She went to the cupboard and retrieved another wine glass. "How long have you been with Myles now—six, eight years?"

"Almost seven," he said. They had been dating only briefly when his father passed.

Estelle poured herself some Pinot Grigio. "Speaking of marriages and divorces, you know, you two can get married now. What's the hold up?"

Tate's face felt a little warm from the wine and maybe, from the sun beaming through the window over the sink. He leaned toward his sister, clinked his glass into hers. "Actually, we already are."

She gasped. "What?"

Their mother came into the kitchen. "Stell, Tate, come out here and meet my friends. Where's Lisa?"

Estelle blinked, swallowed, blinked again. "She went to call Jim. One of the kids has a fever. Luna, I think."

"Oh, that's a shame." She put her hand on the corner of the counter, and her new ring announced itself in the sun.

Tate could smell his mother's perfume, something powdery. Up close, the white dress shimmered, studded with tiny, jewel-like embellishments on the bodice, and on the edges of the scalloped sleeves. The skirt, a loose column, came down just below her knees. Even he had to admit—it was a fabulous dress, perfect for her figure and the occasion. She had never looked her age, and she didn't look seventy now.

"You look great, Mom," he said.

She was surprised. "Thank you, honey." She reached over and squeezed his forearm. "I'm so glad you're here."

Estelle picked up the tray and balanced it against her hip. "And now, I'll be summoning my old waitressing skills." Before she met her ex-husband and dropped out of junior college, she had worked the dinner shift at a local deli.

"You were a terrible waitress," Tate said.

His mother lightly slapped his arm. "She was excellent at that job," she said.

And just like that, he remembered this tendency of hers, to amplify any of their achievements or skills, as though the truth wasn't enough.

"Grab those napkins and be my assistant," Estelle said to Tate, glaring.

And like the obedient baby brother he still was, he followed her.

———

"SHE FAVORS MONICA, don't you think?" A woman with a kindly face approached them, trailed by her husband, who held both of their wine glasses. She peered up at Estelle's face, assessing. "Same eyes, exactly. And you've got your mother's slim build. Beautiful."

"Thank you," Estelle said. "This is my brother, Tate. He favors our father."

The husband raised his eyebrows but said nothing.

"Hand them a napkin, Tate." She lowered the tray. "Would you like a canape?"

"A what? Why, yes. Thank you." The woman loaded three onto her napkin while the husband looked helplessly on, still holding the wine glasses. "Your mother is one of the kindest souls I've ever met. Isn't that right, Bob?"

Estelle smiled. "That's nice of you to say."

"I mean it. She brought me dinner for a week when Bob had his fall. She's the backbone behind our women's group, always thinking of a way to do something good for someone."

"You have a women's group?" Tate asked.

She nodded, chewing bread and salmon. "Somewhat unofficial, but your mother's the leader, that's for sure. Such a good woman. We wish her every happiness, don't we, Bob?"

As Tate followed Estelle around the room, handing out napkins and meeting the people now in his mother's life, he thought about his parents' old life, the house in St. Charles with the creaky staircase and storm door in the back. The neighborhood parties when they were growing up: Fourth of July, Labor Day, birthdays and graduations. Their mother had been in a group in St. Charles, too, also informal and comprised of mothers she'd met through the years. They lunched and shopped together and probably commiserated about teenagers and husbands. She played tennis on Thursdays and taught Sunday school for years. In middle age, she and their father went with other couples on trips—Mexico and Ft. Lauderdale, a river cruise down the Mississippi. Another person, another entire life.

And he remembered that weekend before his college graduation, when he came home determined to share two big announcements: his new job and his new boyfriend. He'd been so worried about his father, his gruff, manly, police officer father. But Tate's father had borne it stoically, actually didn't seem surprised at all. He put his large hand on Tate's shoulder, nodding as he listened. It was Tate's mother who'd gone into almost-hysterics, making threats and denials, crying and cursing. What Estelle and even Lisa didn't understand was that he wasn't upset, after all these years, about that day. Sure, it had hurt his feelings, but his mother had come to him afterwards, apologizing, promising to try. What they didn't understand was that day had been only the tip of the iceberg. Because although Tate and his mother had some semblance of normal relations ever since that day eighteen years ago, they'd never recovered the relationship they'd had before it. They talked about work, about the weather, about houses and clothing and food and trips and bills and everything that wasn't about anybody Tate might be seeing, or caring about, or loving. He supposed it was how people felt when they've lost a spouse and over time, everyone stops mentioning them, as if that person never existed. In his case, it was as if that aspect of himself no longer existed, at least to her. They used to be close, and then, they just weren't. Every Christmas when he couldn't mention a boyfriend, every family event he attended alone, only drove the nail in further and further. And now, he had a husband—a husband!—and because of this *thing* with his mother, he was excluding Myles from this entire part of himself, his family. He'd had a wedding without his sisters, something he could never have imagined and still could hardly believe, even now.

———

TATE HAD GONE OUT to the front yard to have a cigarette. He sat on the metal gliding rocker under the front window, rocking just enough to avoid the squeaking sound that came when he pushed too far.

"There you are." Lisa opened the screen door and let it shut with a bang. She was built like Estelle, like their mother, but was more fluid, more at ease with herself. Her hair was darker, more like Tate's. She sat next to him on the swing.

"How's Luna?" he asked.

She sighed. "It's the baby, Stella. She had a fever, and Jim was freaking out. His mother is there now."

"She's okay though?"

"Oh, yeah. Kids get lots of fevers." She pushed her hair back from her forehead. "Probably if this were Dax at two, I would have jumped on a plane. But this is my third time around."

"An old pro."

"Hey! Leave out the 'old' part! Besides, someone I know recently turned forty."

"And thanks for that reminder," he said.

For a few moments, they swung. He took an occasional drag from his cigarette, which was almost finished.

"Sometimes, I still miss smoking," Lisa said. She had quit before her first pregnancy.

"Want one?"

"Jim would kill me." She extended her long legs and rotated her feet to crack her ankles.

"The human nutcracker," he said. "Please don't do your neck."

She laughed. "What time is dinner? Did Mom say?"

"Five o'clock. Retirement dinner time."

"I thought I'd melt during the ceremony. Thank God it was short." She looked at him. Her eyes were darker blue than Estelle's, more like navy. "Do you like George?"

"He seems okay. I haven't talked to him much."

"He's cheerful. I like that."

Tate got up and dropped the cigarette, twisting his heel on the concrete. Then he picked up the stub and held it. "Listen, Lisa, I have to tell you something before Estelle—"

"She told me."

He rolled his eyes. He'd never understand the workings of female communication—its speed and urgency.

"When did you do it?" she asked. "How?"

He came back to the swing, sat down. "It was small, only a few friends. We had it outside, at a park, then dinner at a restaurant."

"When?"

"We've been together so long we didn't think it was a big deal. Myles didn't have any family there. Well, only his brother because he lives so close."

She had crossed her arms over her chest. "When?"

"That summer before we took the trip to San Diego." He looked down. "That was our honeymoon."

"Almost two years." She let that sink in, then put her hand on his shoulder. "I'm happy for you, really. I can't say I'm not a little hurt, but I understand. At least, I'm trying to understand. Estelle and I have always been there for you. Couldn't you have told us?"

"I'm sorry."

They glided, tentatively and with small movements, on the swing. Lisa inhaled and stood up. "I want to hear all about it, some other time. Today is for Mom. The caterer should be arriving soon, and I should see what needs to be done." She pulled back her shoulders, made a face he'd seen many, many times on the women in his family, and went inside.

———

THE CAKE SAT on a table inside the house, having been brought in from the back sunroom when it started to glisten. Tate stood admiring the delicate piping around the edges of each level, the intricate fleur-de-lis pattern etched on the top layer. This, along with the dress, his mother had gotten right. He wondered if George had been in charge of the tacky arch with the fake flowers.

As though on cue, his mother's new husband came in from the yard. He took off his hat—sort of a half-cowboy, half-gardening thing—and his face spread into a wide grin. It was his most natural expression; in fact, his face had deep grooves from years and years of smiling.

"Everything all right?" George asked.

Tate stepped back from the cake. "Just getting out of the heat. My Midwestern blood isn't used to it."

George smiled even wider, which Tate wouldn't have thought was possible. "But you have the humidity," he said.

A burst of laughter came from outside, and they both looked over, where Tate's mother stood with the three ladies who'd been discussing the red dress earlier in the day. They were as animated as young women at a bar, those four matrons holding their wine glasses and erupting in laughter, again and again. Tate watched as his mother spoke quite animatedly, keeping them rapt throughout whatever story she was telling, pausing here and there for effect, at one point putting her hand over her chest and bending over slightly, at another point, acting out some sort of silly walk. At the end of the story, the three women hooted and chuckled, covering their mouths. He'd never seen his mother like that, commanding attention.

"I'm a lucky man," George said.

Tate turned to look at him.

"My wife, my first wife, has been gone for twelve years," he said. "Cancer."

"I'm sorry," Tate said.

"Thank you. Your mother is a gift, the best gift to me. My second chance."

"I hope you'll be very happy," he said, feeling lame for saying something so cliché.

George nodded and flashed his impossible-to-dislike smile. "We will."

He seemed so certain, so earnest. There was a crease across his forehead from the hat and even that, Tate noticed, was kind of adorable.

"She misses you," George said. "I hope you don't mind that I tell you."

Tate's hand went for his cigarettes, instinctively. "It's okay," he said. "I'll be right back." And he went outside for air.

————

THEY SAT in the backyard on lawn chairs George had pulled from their mother's shed before he left to go back to his own house. In chivalrous fashion, he had insisted on staying there until they all left. Besides, he said, he had family of his own visiting.

Everyone had slept in the morning after the wedding, and

they woke to cinnamon French toast, crisp bacon, and coffee, all courtesy of the bride. Estelle chastised their mother for cooking before they scarfed everything down. In the afternoon, their mother and Lisa both went in to take naps. Lisa seemed to be enjoying having a room to herself, away from noisy children. Tate took charge of dinner and drove to three grocery stores before he found one called AJ's Fine Food, where they had the arugula, shallots, and goat cheese he needed to make his favorite salad. He had planned to make some kind of pasta, but AJ's had a wood-fired oven for pizza, so he ordered everyone their favorite—or at least, what used to be their favorite—pies. The pizzas hadn't compared to what he could get in Chicago, but they weren't bad. And now, they lounged on chairs, post-dinner, well into their second bottle of wine. The sky was a riot of color as the sun set. Tate had forgotten that about Arizona.

"Summer plans," Estelle said. "Anyone?"

Lisa shifted in her seat. "We're going to come down here. Right, Mom?"

"We'd love that."

"I'm thinking maybe late July, or is that the hottest possible time?"

Their mother chuckled and looked for a moment, in the orange dusk, decades younger. "There is no time between May and September that doesn't have the potential to be very hot."

"The kids will love the water park," Lisa said.

"I'm taking a trip in June to Florida," Estelle said. "Food and wine festival in Coral Gables."

"That's a beautiful place," their mother said.

Lisa crossed one leg over the other. "What about you, Tate? Any plans? Anything big going on?" She raised an eyebrow.

He swallowed a huge gulp of Cabernet and cleared his throat. "I'm not sure yet. I do have some vacation time. What about you and George, Mom?"

"Well, honey, we're thinking of taking George's RV on a trip. I'd like to come to Illinois and visit you kids."

"When are you doing that?" Lisa asked.

"Not sure yet, maybe August."

"We have space for an RV," Estelle said. "I've been thinking about moving into a smaller house, actually, but won't do it until the boys are settled."

"I'd like to see your apartment, Tate," their mother said.

He looked at her. "Not many places to park an RV in Chicago."

"Yes, that's true."

Lisa set down her wine glass, too hard, on the glass table next to her chair. "Oops," she said, laughing. Her face was flushed. "You should go up to the Dells, Mom."

They all grew quiet, remembering the many trips they'd taken as a family to the campgrounds just over the border in Wisconsin. They rented a cabin, and a boat their dad would drive uncomplainingly for days, towing them on inner tubes and water skis.

Tate thought about the week his father passed away, the rushed trip down to Arizona and the devastation on his mother's face. She had tried to make amends since then, he knew she had. She was almost always the one who called to check in, and she had mentioned on several occasions coming to the city for a visit. Each time, he evaded her. He wasn't sure why. Was he purposely nursing his resentment?

Estelle went into the house and came out with a radio. Soon, music played, some sort of jazzy station, probably chosen to please their mother. The night was clear and still. They listened while their mother started talking about George's family, his two daughters and how nice they were, how wonderful everyone had been at the wedding. Lisa started tapping her foot to the beat, and Tate watched her, trying to figure out how well she was handling the wine. She'd always been the lightweight of the family.

"—and she tried to catch the vase before it fell, but there was water all over the table, all over the floor." Tate tuned back in as his mother finished a story, something about an accident. "Because without us knowing," she said, "that thing had been leaking like a sieve."

Lisa laughed in a loud spurt. "Oh, Mom, no one says 'sieve' except you."

"I say it," Estelle said. "It's like a colander."

"Or a person who can't keep a secret," Tate said.

They all looked at him.

Their mother went into the house for a third bottle of wine, and by the time she came back out, he and Lisa were dancing across the small lawn.

"Twirl him," Estelle called out.

Because Tate had never been given the lead, not once. Not when he was a little boy and subject to the whims of his older sisters, and not now, a grown man dancing in his elderly mother's back yard. Soon, she and Estelle joined them. They were good together, their mother showing Estelle steps she must have remembered from dancing with their father, or when she was a girl. Or maybe she and George had occasion to dance, even now.

Tate let Lisa lead him onto the patio, where they stopped to drink more wine, then back onto the grass. When a saxophone solo took over one of the numbers, Lisa mimed playing, and they all laughed. He thought maybe they were all a little drunk by then.

Something changed in the air, and abruptly, Lisa stopped dancing. Everyone stopped and turned in the direction she was looking.

"Jim! What in the—" She ran towards her husband, who had just stepped out of the house.

Behind him was Estelle's eldest, Greg, taller than Tate had remembered and sporting a beard that was more intent than facial hair.

Their mother moved to embrace her grandson while Estelle stood, thunderstruck.

And then Greg stepped aside, and there was Myles.

"Don't stop partying on our account," Jim said. He was a tall, barrel-chested guy, with a booming voice that cut through the night. He hugged his wife, then his mother-in-law. "Sorry we missed the wedding, Mom. After I talked to Lisa yesterday, I couldn't understand why I hadn't come in the first place. My mom can handle the kids for a couple of days. This is an important event."

Greg chuckled. "Uncle Jim called and offered me a free ticket. It was forty-three degrees outside, so I said yes."

Estelle had finally reached her son. "I'm happy to see you." Her eyes were watery.

It had never occurred to Tate that it might be difficult for Estelle to be at these events alone, but it had obviously occurred to Jim.

Myles came forward. "Do you remember me, Mrs. Hernandez?"

Their mother looked confused but smiled. "Of course I do, Myles. But I'll still be Monica Langley. I've had that name too long to change now."

"Oh, I'm sorry." He looked down, and his reddish-brown hair fell into his eyes in a way Tate always found irresistible.

"Nothing to be sorry about," she said. "I'm pleased you're here. Estelle, we need more glasses."

"I'll get some. Come with me, Greg."

Jim grabbed Lisa's hand. "Let's dance. We only have forty-two more child-free hours."

Tate nudged Myles in the shoulder. "Were you offered a free ticket, too?"

He looked over without expression. "Among other things."

"Honey," Monica Langley said. "For God's sake, get a chair for this man, who's traveled all this way to see you. And a glass of wine." She walked over, sat down, and picked up her own glass. Suddenly, she looked a little fatigued from the events of the weekend.

"Grandma," Greg said, poking his head outside. "Do you have room for all of us?"

"You can sleep on the sofa," she said. "Put your Uncle Jim's bag in the back bedroom, and whatever Myles brought in the front one. And then get out here and tell me what you've been doing."

Tate was sleeping in the front bedroom, as his mother well knew. Slowly, he walked over and took a seat next to Myles. He watched as his mother called out encouragement to Jim and Lisa, still waltzing underneath the tacky arch. At night, in the muted light from the porch, it looked quite romantic. Tate leaned back in the lawn chair, feeling suddenly tired himself.

Overhead, the black sky still twinkled an impossible number of stars, and the radio still issued the type of jazzy, upbeat music their mother had always enjoyed. Tomorrow, she'd get up and cook for everyone, and Estelle would scold her, and at some point, Lisa and Jim would sneak away for an afternoon "nap."

Tate took a deep breath and let it out, counting as he'd trained himself to do. He looked around the yard at each familiar, mysterious face. In the morning, the desert sun would put them all into stark focus. Tomorrow, he'd head back to the city. And with any luck, Myles would still be by his side, putting up with his stubbornness and imperfections, just like everyone else.

DRIFTWOOD

HE APPEARED against the backdrop of the shadowy Tehachapi Mountains, a blurred form amongst the Joshua trees and tumbleweed in the foreground. From this great distance, the peaks were gray and hazy, saturated with blue from the cloudless sky, quite indistinct in comparison to the expanse of desert that stretched to meet them. A study in browns, her desert, from the abundant brush in varying shades of dryness to the sand underneath; this singular color scheme cloaked the entire valley in which Jackie had lived for fifty-two years.

She strained her eyes, leaning forward at the kitchen window, and watched as the man—she was sure it was a man—ambled along, hunched forward, stopping now and then. Her abdomen pressed against the sink, and she was careful to avoid the tender section. It was a shallow soreness; she'd lived through worse pains.

The man had stopped to crouch down, and she stood on her tiptoes, straining to see him. Her eyes followed the line of the old service road to where a white pick-up was parked a way down. Back when they'd had animals—horses, chickens, dogs—Ken would bring supplies down that narrow passage, but he hadn't used it for years. Occasionally, local kids parked back there to drink or be alone. Once, Jackie watched a group of four boys explore the small, dilapidated barn which, by some miracle of nature, was still standing. More of a shed really, it leaned dangerously to the west. Many times over the years, she'd asked Ken to tear it down or have someone do it, but he didn't worry over it, he said.

Ken worked an occasional Saturday, and on this one, he'd been gone since early morning. Like her, he'd had the same job since they met almost twenty years ago. When he was younger, he helped maintain and deliver rental equipment to homes and job sites, anything from generators to concrete mixers to large-scale landscaping and construction tools. On his time off, he built things and worked outside at his house, this house, which was now Jackie's, too. He'd injured his shoulder falling from a horse, and she'd been his physical therapist. She remembered the first time he took off his shirt, her hands on his muscular shoulder, rotating it gently while he tried not to wince. The electricity, the heat. These days, he worked inside, taking orders and keeping inventory.

Outside, the man moved closer to his truck and without thinking, Jackie fairly leapt toward the door and was half-way down the steps before she realized she'd forgotten her flip flops. Back outside, she squinted in the afternoon sun. She made her way across their land, a mess of weeds and debris where there used to be a modest lawn, a swing set, perennials in wooden holders next to a coiled hose. It had to be ninety-five degrees already. Sweat was forming under her breasts, and she wondered about the large bandage across her ribcage; she'd have to change it later. She shielded her eyes from the sun and kept going.

The man was opening a tarp stretched over some type of frame so that it looked like a tent covering the bed of the truck.

His arms disappeared under the white fabric, then his head. Soon, he popped back up.

She passed the clearing where they'd buried four Labradors. The last, her favorite, a black beauty called Serena whose devotion to Jackie had made Ken jealous. His dog had been Zeus, his first child, really, before he met Jackie. None of the other dogs had ever warmed to him as much.

The man was tying the tarp back down, and Jackie was close enough now to see the bulk of him, broad shoulders and thick forearms. "Hello!" she called, but he didn't seem to have heard her. Dirt was caked around her toes, and flurries of dust had risen in her wake. She looked down, noticing now thick thighs in tight Capri pants, the stain of strawberry jam at the hem of her blouse. She reached up to smooth her hair. Her dad had never made a big deal about clothing, what to wear or whether it was clean or not. She'd learned from other girls and their mothers about things like appearance, neatness, and fashion. Even so, she often reverted to her childhood nonchalance.

The man noticed her now and stood rooted at the spot. Details emerged as Jackie drew nearer: his tight, white tee shirt, worn jeans with a full knee missing, some type of bandanna keeping the dark blonde hair out of his eyes.

"Hello," she said again when she stood at the edge of the old path.

"Afternoon," he said.

Her eyes went immediately to his right arm, which was covered in tattoos. A sleeve, they called it. She had learned this only recently.

He stepped forward, squinting. "Am I trespassing?"

"What? Oh, no," she said. "Well, yes." She smiled.

"Rye Granger," he said, extending his hand. "Rye, like the whiskey."

Jackie thought she had never heard a better name. She'd

known a Butch Granger in school. Baseball player, also tall and blonde. Last she heard, Butch went off to someplace in the Midwest for college, to play third base. He was one of those popular, talented kids who seemed to have everything going for him, no limits to what he might do. They hadn't been friends. In all these years, she'd never thought about him, not once. She shook Rye's hand, which was large and warm and slightly sandy. Across the heated air, his scent reached her nostrils: salt, black licorice, leather.

"Sorry," he said. Reaching back, he pulled a white handkerchief from his pocket and handed it to her.

"No," she said. "It's fine." She wiped her hand on her pants.

"I didn't catch your name," he said.

"Jackie," she said, leaving off her last name. He isn't much older than Stu, she rebuked herself. Stu, your son.

Rye looked towards the mountains, then back at her. His eyes flickered to her chest, but she was used to that. A friend's mother had taken her to buy her first bra when she was ten, after discussing the situation with her dad in hushed tones. Jackie had lived with her large breasts for so long, she couldn't even muster much resentment anymore.

Rye shoved two fingers into the front pocket of his jeans. "Is that your house?" he asked, lifting his head towards it.

"Yes," she said, without thinking.

"How long have you lived here?"

"Why?"

He extended his forefinger and beckoned her and again, without thinking, she went toward him. He watched her close the distance, his eyes searching hers, until she had to look away. Amidst the images crowded onto his arm, she noticed a bearded figure with long hair, in some sort of draped outfit, glaring into the distance.

"Let me show you something," he said. Reaching into the

open driver's window, his tee shirt rode up to expose a couple of inches of lower back. When he stood back up, he was holding a folded sheet of paper, which he opened and spread onto the hood of the truck.

It was a map, its ink faded and hard to make out.

"Did you know there used to be a natural creek here?" he asked.

She bent over the drawing to look where he was pointing. The map was old; she couldn't make sense of it.

"Around 1750, this area had a major drought, and much of the natural water dried up." He straightened, blocking the sun from her face. "If you know how to look, you can see the curve in the land, the impression where the water used to flow." He gazed across the desert, but all Jackie saw was the same dirt, the same brush and weeds. She couldn't imagine this land ever having had a water source, but she didn't want to offend him.

"I'm an artist," he told her. "I make different kinds of art, from all sorts of things, but what really turns me on is finding something with some history, a past."

Jackie turned and leaned her backside against the truck; the metal burned through her capris, but she stayed. "What are you looking for out here?"

He grinned. "Anything left high and dry by that creek. Animal shells, bones, driftwood. I guess you could say I'm also an archaeologist, by way of art."

Jackie looked at her watch. She visited her dad every day, without fail, at two o'clock. It was a quick drive from work during her lunch hour, and she went on the weekends, too. He was in a rehab place in Lancaster, bed-bound for the past two months, getting weaker by the day. After his stroke, Jackie watched him change from a strapping, outdoorsy man to an immobile shadow of himself. Often, she went to his house and wandered through the rooms. Many times, she made plans to start cleaning it out, but she left each time, overwhelmed. They hadn't yet cleaned out most of her mother's things, and she'd been gone for four years already. Her brothers were no help, living as they did out-of-state and being as they had always been, incompetent and selfish. You're being unkind, she told herself.

"Who is that person on your arm?" she asked Rye.

He looked down and turned his forearm slightly. "Zeus," he said. "God of sky and thunder."

Somehow, she had known he'd say that. "We had a dog named Zeus," she said. She looked again at her watch: one thirty-five. "He's buried back here."

"I'm sorry," Rye said, putting his hand on her shoulder, where it caught fire.

Jackie had met her first husband, Stu, in high school. They'd dated throughout their junior and senior years—prom, back-seat sessions, the whole deal—and they'd gotten married two years after that. Jackie finished her physical therapy program while Stu worked as a security guard. They bought a little ranch-style home on the east side of town and made payments on a brand new, blue hatchback. And when they were ready to start a family, they painted the smallest bedroom and bought a crib and changing table. Ten months later, Stu Jr. was born, and two years after that, Stu Sr. was killed on his way home from work by a drunk driver.

"It's strange," she said. "I was thinking about that dog right after I saw you, and here you are with that tattoo." She thought, also, about the way she'd spent the morning, the pulsing ache under her shirt.

Rye lifted his hand from her shoulder and slowly folded up the map. The motions made his chest contract under the tee shirt. "Do you know what I was thinking about, before I saw you?" he asked.

She shook her head, although he wasn't watching her.

"I had a girlfriend once," he said, "a blonde like you. She was a girl of many talents. And when I saw you storming your way across that yard—"

"I wasn't storming."

"A sunbeam," he said, looking at her. "Yellow hair blazing."

Jackie had never had trouble getting attention from boys or men. But after Stu's father died, she'd forgotten that side of herself for a good, long while. Stu became her priority, working and caring for him her only purpose. Meeting Ken had caught her completely by surprise. She realized that a great, hungry part of her had been hiding all along. She looked at Rye—the bulk of him, the burn on the back of his neck. "Do you believe in signs?" she asked him.

He came to her then, straddled her legs with his own and grabbed her elbows with his large, rough hands. His face was close enough that she could see the pores on either side of his nose. His teeth were unbearably straight and white. "Jackie," he said. "I believe, without a doubt, in signs of all kinds." Just as suddenly, he gently released her and turned away. He threw the map into the truck.

Stunned, loose, tingling, Jackie leaned against the truck. She cleared her throat. "Would you like to come to the house for a sandwich? It's better if you move your truck and park in front."

Rye motioned with his head towards the passenger seat. "Hop in," he said. His maddening blue eyes glowed like neon. "I also strongly believe in sandwiches, all kinds of sandwiches."

———

JACKIE PICKED up the sculpture of the bird once more. Smooth and cool to the touch, it had been carved from discovered wood and attached to a mahogany stand. What she found most interesting about the sculpture, about all four of the objects Rye had brought in from his truck, was that they weren't actual, realistic representations. The bird was obviously a bird, but because it *suggested* a bird. There were two narrow spans of wood that rose from the main, central portion, and these seemed like wings. There was the conical tip that suggested a beak, the rounded bottom, the grooves like feathers throughout the grain.

"Can you tell what it's going to be before you start?" she asked.

Rye swallowed the last bit of his sandwich and nodded.

She had heated up roast pork from last night's dinner, raked it into strips and added barbecue sauce. She offered him a beer and when he accepted, she opened one for herself, thinking as she always did about the medication and how she was supposed to avoid alcohol. But she didn't take the pills often, and she was a moderate drinker. In fact, she'd been thinking about getting rid of the medicine all together. She wasn't feeling anxious anymore, at least she wasn't today.

They sat across from each other at the kitchen island. Ken had let her redecorate as a gift for their tenth anniversary, and Jackie had chosen black leather stools to match the granite slab with its depths of gray, black, and silver. Lately, the kitchen had started to seem outdated. "Do you want another beer?" she asked, although Rye's was still a third full.

"I'd better not," he said. "I've got some driving left to do."

She set the wooden bird on the counter. "I never asked where *you* live."

He leaned back. "I'm between living arrangements at the moment. Not homeless but home free."

"Where do you sleep?"

"I've got a twin mattress in the back of the truck. Friends who let me crash occasionally."

She watched, waiting for him to say more.

In a long swig, he finished the beer. His eyes had a pleasing softness now as he looked at her. Over the course of their lunch, she'd gotten used to his gaze. It had been a while, she supposed, since someone had looked at her so intently, had listened so closely. Of course, people *listened*. She went to work and spoke to patients and coworkers; she came home and talked about Ken's day with him. But this man seemed interested in her at a level that probed something deep within her, like a tongue looking for a lost tooth.

"I used to live here but mostly grew up in Arizona," he said. "Little town called Roosevelt, near Scottsdale. But my grand-mother lives here, always has. My uncle passed, and we had his funeral yesterday."

"I'm sorry for your loss," Jackie said.

"Thanks." He crossed his arms over his chest. "My uncle used to watch me sometimes when I was little. He was much younger than my mom—his sister—so he was sort of like an older brother to me. Played baseball with me, stuff like that. Then we moved away, and I saw him like most people do, family events, weddings and funerals."

She thought again of Butch Granger but didn't ask. "What are your plans?" she asked instead.

His forehead wrinkled. "Plans?"

"You know, for life. Where do you see yourself in ten years?" She shrugged. "Isn't that something people ask?"

Slowly, his mouth spread into a grin. "I'm more of a day-to-day kind of person, always have been. Drives my mother crazy, because she's been worrying about me for thirty-eight long years. Her words."

"Does she like your art?"

"She does, despite herself."

Jackie picked up the horse sculpture, her favorite. She ran her hand over the gleaming haunches, circled one back leg with her thumb and forefinger. Her dad loved horses, an interest discovered later in life after she married Ken. He used to come over and help Ken out back. He used to be tall and solid as a tree. Jackie remembered looking out the same kitchen window, watching him lead Jackson, Stu's favorite horse, around the path now overgrown with wild plants. Stu, sitting upright and listening carefully to his grandfather. Ken, somewhere in the distance, working, but keeping an eye on the proceedings. Stu was seven when they married, and he loved Ken like a father, which is what her husband had been. She couldn't complain about that, not one bit.

"My son lives in Boise," she said. "Idaho." Her throat ached, thinking of it.

Rye's eyes sparkled. "I know where Boise is, Jackie." Slowly, he wiped his mouth with the back of his hand.

Jackie was a little sleepy from the beer. She shook her head, stood up. Had she taken the medicine that morning? "Your sculptures are wonderful," she said. "I like them all, the bird, the —what is it, a seal?"

He nodded, watching her.

She stroked the back of the seal, which was a complete, undivided piece of wood, scrubbed clean as glass. "My mother died when I was five," Jackie said. "I never knew her, not really. Your uncle, he was good to you?"

"Yes."

"That's nice." She thought of her dad, lying underneath the beige blanket the nurses always pulled up under his chin, even when it was too warm. She thought of her brothers and the tents they made from old sheets and blankets, flashlight beams bouncing underneath, but they always kept her out. She liked watching them anyway, liked when they were laughing instead of fighting, liked listening to their bragging. She'd been surrounded by boys and men her entire life, she realized.

"Jackie."

She felt warmth on the back of her neck and knew that Rye was behind her, had stood and walked around the island and now waited for her to notice, to turn. She inhaled, her chest straining painfully. Her throat was burning. Her hair had once been vibrant copper, deep and shiny as a new penny. Now it was lighter and flecked with gray, which she had covered up every six weeks to the tune of ninety dollars. At night, she soaked her feet and used a heating pad on her lower back while she watched television with Ken. Her son had moved eight hundred miles away, and her dad was vanishing before her eyes. That goddamn drunk driver. Loss after loss after loss. Most nights, Ken started snoring in his recliner before whatever they were watching was over. He'd stopped working outside, had stopped doing anything besides going to work and coming home. The animals, all gone, her brothers, lost long before they moved away. Twice recently, patients had asked to see another therapist; she'd been called in to discuss her "current situation." She hadn't even told Ken —when could she? Between his naps and the times he simply stared past her at the dinner table? The house needed work, but neither of them seemed to care. She had moments of confusion, of fear. She'd seen a doctor, the one who gave her the prescription that was supposed to be a short-term fix; she had been refilling it for the better part of a year. Her dad's stubborn, beating heart and slack jaw. The house. Her aching back. The warm fur of the dogs, the click of their nails. How she missed the dogs! Her husband didn't desire her anymore or at least, he never made any efforts. There had been no announcement, no problem or event. Slowly, they'd just stopped. Everything had stopped, was in a perpetual state of slowly stopping.

Jackie picked up the sculptures, holding all four against her chest, where they poked her here and there. The last one, a squirrel, was tucked under her chin. Without facing Rye, she moved away from his warmth and walked to the front door.

He followed and let her out.

She passed under his outstretched arm and made her way towards the truck, which he'd parked in the shade of the old elm tree next to the garage. After he pulled back the tarp, opened the tailgate, and took the sculptures one by one from her hands, her eyes finally met his. Then she turned and slowly—although with much more agility than she would have imagined—climbed under the tarp and onto the mattress spanning the length of the truck bed.

He stood for a moment looking at her before he moved aside the small box holding the sculptures and joined her under the tented tarp.

———

JACKIE'S HAND was steady as she lit the tapered candles. She'd found them in a drawer, thrown in with lots of other things she didn't use anymore. She used to put out the candles at Christmastime. Ken used to help her decorate the house from top to bottom.

At the stove, the pasta cooked underneath a cloud of steam. She glanced at the timer and peeked at the dinner rolls browning in the oven. She'd poured herself some wine already, thinking again about the medication, only she'd dumped the remaining tablets into the toilet an hour ago. Already, she second-guessed that decision.

Ken's car purred into the driveway. Looking at the table, she realized how stupid the candles were. It was summer, light outside until after eight o'clock. Still, she thought they added something. She wanted to make an effort. She wanted to try.

Through the sheer curtains, she watched as Ken heaved

himself from the car and turned to shut the door. When had he gotten so old, so out-of-shape? He stood for a moment, looking back at the street, then trudged toward the house. On the top step of the porch, she clearly saw him hesitate, take a long, deep breath, and pull his shoulders back before he entered. As though he dreaded walking in.

He took in the tablecloth, the wine, the candles, and looked up to see her in a clean blue sundress. She'd pulled her hair back on one side with a barrette. "Jackie?" he said.

"I made dinner," she said, turning back to the kitchen.

"How soon will it be ready?"

"Whenever you are."

"Let me clean up," he said.

She listened as he walked down the hallway and opened the door to their bedroom. He still used the master bathroom, but she'd moved all her toiletries into the guest bath. It seemed much easier than sharing sink space and a shower with him. What had happened to them? A wave of fear passed over her. Why had she thrown away the pills? She thought about an aunt and uncle of hers, who had lived in separate bedrooms for decades. She used to think it was terrible.

The nurse from the rehab place had called earlier, while Jackie was in the shower. She said that her dad had a new rash on his arm. They think it was caused by the IV tape used; sometimes it happened to patients with certain sensitivities. They didn't want her to be alarmed when she saw it, they said. And of course she felt guilty for missing her visit, although she doubted her dad would even notice, or notice the rash, or anything else that happened in that dreadful little room. Loss after loss after loss.

Jackie swallowed the last of her wine and turned off the stove. The water around the pasta bubbled, smaller and smaller, until it stopped. She pulled the rolls out of the oven and dropped them into a basket. Then she walked down the hall, looking for Ken, stopping briefly to admire the wooden horse on the entry table by the front door. She'd take it tomorrow to show her dad.

In the bedroom, the curtains were pulled shut, save for a slice of muted, orange sunlight that cut the bed into two equal halves. The bathroom was bright, all shiny surfaces, and Ken stood at the mirror, brushing his teeth.

"What are you doing?" she asked. "We're going to eat."

He shrugged and seemed embarrassed. She smelled a whiff of cologne, too. Maybe the dress, the candles—he thought something would happen. A rush of tenderness rushed through her. Her husband, her Ken.

"I have to talk to you," she said. "I did something today."

He spit a stream of water and wiped his mouth with a towel, all the while watching her in the mirror.

Slowly, she reached down and grabbed the bottom of her dress. She pulled it up and over her head and stood behind him in her bra and panties. A fresh bandage glared white just under the bottom right side of her ribcage.

"What is that?" he asked, turning.

Carefully, she loosened the corner of the bandage and pulled it off. She saw herself in the mirror, the expansive breasts, wider hips, the same good legs. She looked at her husband.

His eyes had widened, and she tried to gauge his reaction as it changed, gradually, from surprise to confusion to something else. He turned and leaned down to see more closely. When he straightened up, he grabbed her by the shoulders and looked her right in the eyes. "I love it," he said. "I sincerely, without a doubt, love it."

"You do?"

He pulled her against him, and she could feel him trembling. "Yes," he said.

She laughed, and he laughed, and they held each other like that, shaking a little. After some time, she put her dress back on, and he put his arm around her shoulder.

"Let's go eat," he said. "I want to hear all about it. Did it hurt? How did you decide what to get? Where did you go, that place on Sierra Highway? Do you think I should get one?"

Jackie leaned her head on his shoulder and let herself be led down the hallway, listening to the unchanging, familiar sound of his voice, looking around the house at all they had, and making all sorts of promises to herself, and to him, under her breath.

RESONANT BLUE

May

THE FIRST SIGN was the bag of supplies left on the quartz countertop. He didn't recognize it at the time, of course. He didn't walk in after a long day at the building site, an endless day of problems relayed by project managers, accountants, and safety advisors, and think: So this is the first sign. He simply noticed the plastic bag on the otherwise pristine surface and figured she must have meant for him to see it. She had ways of hiding things she didn't want him to know about.

He made a mental note to ask her about the bag, although after the day he'd had, he didn't really care what it was. He knew this was how you make a relationship work—noticing the small things, paying careful attention to the big ones. She stood at the stove, her back turned. The curves, the fiery hair.

Only much later did he trace his troubles back to that Thursday evening, before the interrupted sex, even before she cooked the steak with mushrooms and thyme. Only later did he see that the plastic bag was the first sign.

The house was a modern bi-level overlooking the ocean.

Both floors made the most of the expansive view and salty air; on the first, retractable walls opened to make the place virtually al fresco. He had a large deck built with Ipé hardwood from South America. The pronunciation sounds like ee-pay, which rhymes with we-pay, and that's exactly what he'd done. Through the nose. It wouldn't do for an architect to have a home anything less than stunning, and this one was, after he'd finished renovating. If he were as good at divining the future as he'd become at tracing events backwards, he might have said that the purchase of the house had been a bolt of lightning striking the stagnant sea of his marriage. From there, it was all buzz and detritus.

He'd stripped everything, rebuilt and remodeled. Knocked down partitions, added bells and whistles. Installed walls that moved so he could always get air. In the kitchen, an open design and quartz countertops because granite had become passé. At least, that's what he was told by the hired kitchen consultant, a tall and husky-voiced divorcee he'd slept with for two months.

He set his briefcase next to the plastic bag and thought: Thank God my single days are over.

Brigetta turned towards him. On the stovetop, something brownish simmered, smelling delicious. She continued stirring.

He walked over and nuzzled his face into her hair. "Looks great."

"Internet recipe," she said. "Steak with mushrooms and thyme."

He curved his shoulders around hers, leaning in. "I've got nothing but thyme."

"Funny." She pushed him back with her buttocks. "It's hot."

He moved away as she lifted her hair and pulled it to one side. A few strands fell back down.

They met at a hotel opening. She was one of the art buyers who'd worked on the guest rooms, too junior to take on the lobby. He was there representing the architectural firm, although he didn't have much to do with the hotel. Across the grand ballroom, he'd noticed her flaming hair first, then her smile, then the rest. Later, she seemed surprised that he assumed the deep red color was her own. No one has hair this color, she told him. It reminded him of his first car, a Chevy Nova he took to Earl Scheib for the ninety-nine-dollar paint job. Shimmered like a kaleidoscope up close.

"What's this?" He looked at the bag, proud of himself for asking.

She turned from the stove, pressing a forearm against her sweaty forehead. "Oh! Is it okay if I paint the corner bedroom?"

The house had four bedrooms, three up and one down. Upstairs, an expansive master bedroom, a second that served as his home office, and the other. The third was originally meant to be his office and the larger one for his daughter, Maddie, but she had never moved in. His marriage crumbled as the house was rebuilt, and Maddie stayed with her mother in Agoura Hills. The corner bedroom was the smallest and least remarkable, with no ocean view and serving currently as storage space for Brigetta's unpacked boxes.

She shut off the burner and faced him. "I know what you're going to say, and I will." Reaching into a cupboard, she pulled down a jar of something. "But until I can go through everything, my parents said I could store some of it at the house."

"I don't think—"

"It's done," she said. "They have tons of space in the garage. I'll take the kitchen stuff, the boxes of books."

"We can put shelves in," he said.

"For what, my college textbooks?"

Brigetta had been an art major and then switched to business. Her job as a commercial art buyer had seemed like the perfect merging of the two disciplines, until it wasn't. When they met, she talked about feeling restless and unfulfilled. About exploring her own art or becoming a teacher. Or working at an art museum. Or a gallery. Or doing interior design. She talked about all these things, and it seemed natural for someone her age, and charming, and—if he was honest—exciting to imagine her forging a career, a future. With him. And then she lost her job in a corporate layoff and was still talking about what to do these many months later. Luckily, he had plenty of money and didn't really care what she did.

She stood at the stove, stirring. "I was thinking about getting a paint easel, maybe a chaise lounge. For the room."

He reached over and rifled through the plastic bag. Paint brushes and rollers, painter's tape, wooden stir sticks. She'd thrown in what looked to be twenty or thirty paint sample cards. He turned and put his hands on her hips. "Whatever you want," he said. "But we can hire someone to paint."

"Watch out," she said, pushing him away again. Leaning over, she pulled a steaming, crackling tray of broiled steak from the oven. Her cheeks shone from the heat, her breasts pressed together into glistening cleavage framed by the low V of her pale green tee shirt. She set the meat noisily on the stovetop. "Please, Tony," she said. "I want to do it."

"Whatever you want," he said again. The sight of her, breathing heavily in front of the oven, her scarlet hair tucked behind each ear, the fragrance of the meat and mushrooms, the luxury of the kitchen, the house, the Pacific Ocean bestowing its brininess like a blessing; he remembered later, when he spooled things back to that Thursday evening, to the telltale bag, to the subtleties and the niceties, instead of being alarmed in any way, he remembered thinking he might be the luckiest man on the planet, to have all this, and this, and also, this.

———

June

THE PROJECT WAS AN APARTMENT BUILDING, and it was supposed to be his chance to stretch a bit. The investor was a trust fund kid who, like Brigetta, was also a failed art student. Be creative, he'd said. In a flurry of inspiration, Tony drafted and planned; he hadn't been so excited about a project in years. He took Brigetta to Fiji, and they drank beer and ate fish soaked in coconut and lime. They came back when construction was set to begin. Immediately, problems stacked up. The millwork planned for the entrance and the lobby had to be reordered from another supplier; the local housing authority issued complaints. Normal, minor things at first. But then there were fundamental safety concerns with the plumbing and the jutting, asymmetrical glass balconies, and the corner units that projected out several feet from the rest of the building. They'd had to stall construction in the early phases to let a structural engineering firm reevaluate for earthquake resistance. Even the curlicue, steel decorative sheets he'd planned were in question. Too sharp, too heavy.

Things had gone from bad to worse, and he took it as a sign. After a long, tense meeting with the other partners at the firm, he'd spent several days at home redrafting many of the more artistic elements. He'd been imprudent in his design; he realized that now. He was losing sleep over the thing. Around the office, the project had become somewhat of a joke; Tony's Shangri-la. Of course, they never said it to his face.

He'd just submitted the latest adjustments to the appropriate managers and team and had decided to work from home for the remainder of the day. A brilliant southern California afternoon, the ocean spread like a soaked rug as he maneuvered his Benz around twists and turns. But his mind was on the project. He still wondered, after everything, if he could salvage the curvy, steel parts for the exterior. The only artistic, unspoiled thing from his plan, it seemed.

At the mouth of his driveway, a white pickup was parked backwards, blocking the entrance. He rubbed his burning eyes and cursed. He was so tired. The truck looked vaguely familiar, but he couldn't place it. There were several boxes in the bed, and the tailgate was down. He parked next to the trees lined up for privacy at the front of the lawn.

A young man came down the driveway, his long legs splayed to support a big cardboard box. "Hey, Tony."

It was Brigetta's brother, he realized.

"This is the last," Alex said. He wore tattered jeans, and the hems dragged around his sandals. He looked much like his sister, with the same slim build and sharp features. "We got most of it yesterday."

Yesterday? He wondered why she hadn't mentioned it, then he remembered coming home late after work.

Brigetta appeared in the doorway, holding a smaller container. "Anthony." She came down the steps and squinted up at him in the sunlight. "Remember I said my parents can keep this stuff in their garage?"

He nodded, and she followed her brother to the end of the driveway. From the porch, Tony watched them load the boxes, speaking in low voices.

Brigetta sprinted back up the driveway and stopped before him, out of breath. "I'm going to ride with Alex, and he'll bring me back later," she said.

He imagined the family reunion about to take place, with Brigetta's father happily loading his daughter's things back into the house as her mother supervised. They'd always been polite to him, but never more. Her mother had a way of raising her eyebrows to everything he said, a whimsical, pleasant-enough expression that really meant I will tolerate you until I don't have to anymore.

Brigetta extended her leg and tapped her toe on the ground, pivoting her ankle. She couldn't stand still. She glanced back at the truck, waiting for him to speak.

He nodded. "I'm going to work for a while. Will you be home for dinner?"

"Maybe," she said. "Probably not." Her lips brushed his cheek. "See you later."

He watched her walk away. She moved slowly, but it seemed to take effort, as though she was willing herself not to run. Halfway down the driveway, she turned back. "Don't look in the corner bedroom! I want it to be a surprise."

He raised his hand in farewell, feeling sorry for himself. True, he had planned to work, but an afternoon bedroom session wouldn't have been entirely out of the question. They hadn't seen each other much lately. Brigetta had been spending time at a friend's newly opened boutique. Interior design consulting, she called it, although he expected it was mostly hanging out. She'd leave takeout containers for him in the microwave. A few times, she went to art showings or movies and came in late. He'd been preoccupied with work and tried to remember the last time they'd had sex. There was the night she cooked that steak before the phone call from his ex-wife. No, there'd been another time after that. Still, it wasn't much.

When Alex's truck disappeared around the corner, he went straight up to the corner bedroom. The starkness startled him. The walls were still the same bone white as the rest of the house, and the only furniture in the room was an old, slip-covered recliner he'd been too sentimental to let go. He could see now that it didn't fit in. Near the lone, small window sat the bag of paint supplies, still full. She'd hung up the paint cards with clear tape. The swatches of color made a jagged, horizontal line across one of the longer walls and part of a second. He had to stoop to read them and realized they were hung at her eye level.

Slowly, he walked down the line of cards, reading the names. There were greens: Nurture Green, Recycled Glass; blues: Open Seas, Cloudburst; oranges: Emberglow, Cavern Clay; and an assortment of others. Pale purples, vivid yellows, more blues: Bridgewater, Forget-Me-Not, Resonant Blue. Didn't she have anything in mind? Hadn't she narrowed it down at all?

He stood at the window for a moment. Turning sideways, he watched his reflection as he sucked in his belly. Through the trees, a flicker of color caught his attention amidst the jostling leaves. He remembered the car; he'd have to move it.

July

HE BANGED his arm against the corner of the nightstand as he reached the telephone. "Damn. Hello?"

"Tony, it's Margaret."

He sat up, rubbing his eyes. What time was it? Through the vast window across from his bed, the sun set in a rage of orange and pink.

"Are you there?"

"Yeah."

She sighed, a familiar sound. "It's early. Were you sleeping?"

"A little nap. I haven't been sleeping much lately."

Margaret snickered. "One of the perks of having a girlfriend half your age, I guess."

"She's not—" He walked across the room and turned on the overhead light. "Why are you calling? Is it Maddie?"

"She's fine. I mean, I think she's fine." She paused. "Have you heard from her?"

Tony pictured his ex-wife, perched on the kitchen stool

nearest the phone. She used to twirl the cord around her finger as she talked; the telephone used to be beige with white numbers, hanging from the wall. Cordless phones came and then cellular, and still she sat in the same chair to talk.

"I got an email last week," he told her. "She was in Prague."

"And you didn't think to call me?"

"No, why?"

"We said she could travel to England, France, and maybe up to Amsterdam if there was time, although I was hoping they wouldn't."

"Maybe they changed their minds," he said. Maddie was a responsible kid, always had been, and she was with her best friend, Sara, who was also a great kid. Back in the day, Tony and Margaret had shared barbecues and pool parties, dance recitals and carpools with Sara's parents. Both girls had graduated with honors; both had plans for good colleges. This European trip was their graduation present, a chance to explore before Maddie went up to Berkeley in August and Sara back east.

"This was not a free pass to Europe, courtesy of Mom and Dad!" Margaret's voice quaked. "I've had the hardest time getting a hold of her, Tony."

"You told me that last week," he said. Margaret's calls never seemed to come at a convenient time. During meetings at work, while he listened to a good baseball game on his drive home, or the time she called the house and his cell, over and over, interrupting some great mid-week sex with Brigetta. "I suggested that you email," he said. "Give her some space."

"It's easy for you! Nothing comes back to you."

"What do you mean?"

"You get to be the fun parent. That's easy."

"Margaret, what exactly is the problem? She went to Prague instead of Amsterdam? That's a good thing, isn't it? Remember how fried we got in Amsterdam?" He thought about Margaret of the fringed jacket and hoop earrings, who chased him behind a restaurant in the Jordaan and pulled her shirt over her head. This woman seemed a foreign, twice-removed cousin of that Margaret. Sure, her blonde hair was shorter now, her hips wider. But it was more than that.

"She was supposed to be back tomorrow," she said, "and I did take your advice. In fact, her email today said she's extending the trip to circle back to Spain. She has to see Barcelona, she said."

"Does she have enough money?" he asked.

"The credit card. Is that your only concern?"

He'd been pacing the room, adjusting the blinds, smoothing the bedspread and picking up pillows. In the bathroom, he picked up one of Brigetta's tank tops and noticed the neckline was flecked with bright blue paint. He scratched at one of the spots then threw it into the hamper.

"Tony?"

"Yes."

"Don't you have any questions? Aren't you worried about our eighteen-year-old daughter traveling through Europe alone?"

"She's with Sara. What do her parents say about it?"

"That's the thing. Sara's coming home," she said. "Maddie's staying alone. I think she's met someone, or something's happened."

"Maddie? No. It's probably what she said, a quick trip to Barcelona. She has traveled all over the world with us," he reminded her. "She'll be fine."

Margaret sniffled. "Maybe."

"When will she be back?"

"Another week."

On the glossy, travertine threshold of the shower, Tony noticed a speck of something. A stain of some sort—makeup, shampoo? He leaned over and found that it was affixed. More paint. Blue. He flicked it off easily with a fingernail.

Margaret started reciting all the things that still needed to happen before Maddie could settle into her dorm in Berkeley. Household items to be purchased, clothing to organize, school supplies to acquire. As she talked, he felt his way down the stairs. The house was darkening, moment by moment. He found his cell phone on the kitchen counter and checked for a message from Brigetta. Nothing. She'd gone to a movie with Charlene, the boutique owner. Something foreign in Glendale. Or Pasadena. He couldn't remember.

"You think it's okay?" Margaret asked. "I mean, Maddie having this extra week?"

Tony walked to the edge of the room and pressed a silver button. Magically, majestically, the glass-paned wall opened, and the night pressed in: pastel colors diluting to dark, ocean breeze of salt and form, the static of breaking waves.

"I'll call her," he said.

"Thanks. She's much more forthcoming with you these days, strangely. But will you listen, Tony?"

He heard a clicking sound, then two steady beeps. Margaret's car, he realized, the keys left in the ignition. She wasn't on the kitchen stool after all.

"I mean, really listen," she said. "And let me know, all right?"

"Sure." He inhaled a good-sized portion of the salty breeze. He thought about his ex-wife alone in her house, only the kitchen alighted, that idiot cat weaving through the chair legs.

"And will you pick her up next week at LAX?" she asked. "She's supposed to email the flights."

"Yes," he said, and with his head propped on his fist as he gazed at the meeting of sand and surf, "yes," again, and "yes," to all the rest.

———

HE STOOD at the base of Vista Apartments, squinting up through the scaffolding. The building's exterior was coming along. There were sections with solid walls, and others where his plans were still exoskeleton and intention. They were working on the corner units today, bringing up the modified steel pieces for the balconies.

Tony walked across the street and leaned against the sign in front of the apartment building that faced the project. He gazed up at the nondescript structure. Lacks imagination, he thought, just a stack of boxes. Although he knew what sort of planning went into even that.

He'd just spoken with the project manager who, for once, had nothing but positive reports. Even with the design changes and setbacks, they were on schedule for a pre-Christmas opening. Sixty percent of the units had already been rented, which meant happy, non-interfering owners.

He watched as one of the twisting, shiny pieces of metal was attached to the front of a balcony on the second floor. Sunlight sparked from the surface as it was lifted into place. A new sound cut through the air, a squeal rising above the pounding taking place inside. In a few moments, the decoration was installed, and he exhaled.

His cell phone vibrated in his front pocket. He glanced at the display and answered. In the background, rushing static. She was driving. "Hey, baby," he said.

"Anthony, where are you?"

"Working."

"At home?"

"I'm at the site, the apartments."

Brigetta exhaled. "Oh, okay."

He watched as the workers stopped drilling and stood on the

scaffolding, discussing and pointing. There seemed to be some problem with the steel piece, or maybe not. He hoped not.

"I just wondered," she said.

Now he could hear the radio in the background, hip hop or was it rap? He could never be sure.

"Where are you going?" he asked.

"Stopping by the house. You remember the artist we met, the muralist?"

Across the street, the project manager came out to the sidewalk and stood, arms akimbo, looking up at the workers.

"His name is Leonard," she said. "He's going to stop by and give me some ideas about the room."

"The room," he repeated.

"The guest room. Are you listening?"

"Yeah," he said. "Baby—"

"I can call back," she offered.

"That would be good," he said. "I'm here at the site."

There was a muffled sound, then quiet. One of the workers was leaning over the scaffolding.

"You still there?" he asked.

"I'll tell you everything later," she said.

"What about dinner?"

"I may have to run back to the boutique. The curtains and upholstery fabrics have come in."

"You were there last night." He had reheated some fettucine and fell asleep watching the Dodgers game.

"No," she said. "Last night, I went to that lecture on street murals. I'm on a mural kick, I guess!" She laughed in a weird, short burst. "I'll call you later."

Across the street, the stout project manager had gone back inside. Above, work had resumed. At the furthermost corner of the balustrade, the first of the curving steel pieces remained. It protruded, gleaming and sharp, like a lone eyetooth.

He remembered, then, the postcard on a table near the door, the mural of sheer clouds with a bright blue sky, scattered wingspans and below, an empty bench. The name of some gallery and a date.

"Baby?" he said. But she had already hung up.

August

MADDIE BROUGHT PRESENTS HOME: a colorful, beaded scarf for Brigetta, and a book on Czech architecture for her father. She had insisted on finding them in her bulging suitcase while Tony was parked in a loading zone at LAX, then had been annoyed when he exchanged terse words with a cabdriver.

"There, we're done," Brigetta had said, interceding. "Get in the car, Anthony, and we'll be right there."

He felt the adjustment when they hoisted the heavy luggage into the trunk, then the whoosh when they both climbed into the back seat. He looked at Brigetta in the rearview mirror.

"I'll sit back here," she said. "I want to see what else Maddie brought."

He watched them as he weaved his way into traffic. Their heads were bent over a small box, the tame blonde Maddie had inherited from her mother, the unlikely red of Brigetta's. Both kept their hair long, past their shoulders and parted down the middle. Every woman under thirty seemed to have this same hairstyle, or lack of hairstyle. Sometimes Brigetta would twist hers into a spiraled cone, held with a leather-accented clip. The first time she'd gone home with him she'd worn it like that. He remembered the way she had climbed on him, and the opaqueness of her arms, lifted in the moonlight to unclasp her hair.

"Dad," Maddie said. "Look at this necklace. I bought it at a street fair in Prague. The artist uses pieces of her hair to make tiny ropes and braids and encases the whole thing in glass." She held up a cheap-looking chain with a blob of clear material at the end.

"Why would you want to wear a piece of a stranger's hair?" he asked. It had been two weeks since the email to her mother, not one as Maddie had promised.

She lowered the necklace and handed it to Brigetta. "She makes them with a loved one's hair, you know, if you wanted to take a boyfriend's, or your kid's or something."

Aside from the new, smallish diamond stud in her nostril, Maddie looked more or less the same. It had only been a few weeks, but he imagined that when she'd been gone for months at a time in Berkeley, the changes would intensify. For now, she was the same girl she'd always been: sunshine blonde, with her mother's long torso and dainty hands. She had his brown eyes and full lips and thankfully, not much else. Not that he was bad looking, but it was hard to imagine his type of dark looks, his full eyebrows and ropy arms, the broad face he had to shave sometimes twice a day—to imagine any of this translating to a female form. And yet it had. Maddie seemed to have the best bits from both of her parents.

"What was your favorite place?" Brigetta asked.

"Barcelona," Maddie said. "Without a doubt."

Brigetta sighed. "I knew it. I'd love to go there."

"You have to!" Maddie said. "The weather, the water, La Rambla at night. And, of course, what everyone knows, the decorative tile, the architecture!" She leaned forward in her seat. "We had the best seafood at this tiny place not too far from Playa del Bogatell. That's a beach."

"Who's 'we'?" Tony asked.

Maddie looked down. "I met some people at the hotel," she said. "We hung out a little."

"Have you ever been there?" Brigetta asked him.

"Of course," he said.

"But not as a student," Maddie said. "You went later, something for work."

"Yeah, so?"

"I just think, you know, it's different. It probably would've had a big effect if you'd been younger."

"More mosaic tiles on my buildings?"

"Maybe!" She laughed. "I didn't mean anything by it. But a magical place like that—I'm starting to rethink my own career goals, that's all."

"Really?" The last he'd heard, Maddie was proudly undecided and planning to take an array of liberal arts once she got to Berkeley.

"It opened my eyes. The whole trip, really."

Brigetta reached over the seat and squeezed his shoulder. He caught a whiff of her perfume, sweet and powdery. "But you had that whole semester in France, didn't you, Anthony?" She turned to Maddie. "There's another place I'd like to go. I've been to Paris but nowhere else. You were in the south of France, weren't you?"

Colors flashed before his eyes. "I spent a couple of days in London," he said, "took the ferry to Paris. The host family was in Lyon."

Maddie searched for his eyes in the mirror. "But I thought you never made it there."

The collection of images was minimal, really, after all these years. The Eiffel Tower, a steaming cup of the darkest coffee he'd ever seen, the endless blue around the boat, so much like the Pacific, and yet, hard to fathom the distance he'd come. He remembered the hopefulness of the voyage to the mainland, the deflation of the ride back.

"I was there," he said. "I was there for a week, but then I had to come back."

"That was when his mom died," Maddie said. "I never knew her, obviously."

"Oh," Brigetta said. "I didn't know that."

He glanced back, and she was looking at him oddly. "I'm sure I told you," he said.

"Paris is sublime," Maddie said. "And my God, the food. I gained ten pounds."

"You didn't," Brigetta said. "You're perfect."

The young women chatted away, and Tony listened, happy for the sound and content to be driving. It had been twenty-five years. They'd cleared out his mother's things, and he helped his father make arrangements for his sister, who still lived at home. A carpool with the neighbor, a babysitter after school. The car had been totaled, so there was nothing to do there. His sister finished school and college, got married, and stayed home to raise her kids. His older brother moved to Seattle, where he works and takes his boat out when he's off. A wife, two children. Eventually, his father remarried a nice widow who likes to travel although lately, they'd been home more often. Getting older. It had all turned out okay, Tony reminded himself.

They dropped Maddie at her mother's. Margaret looked tired but happy, and she almost tripped on the porch steps in her rush to get to their daughter. She thanked Tony and gave him a long, speculative look. As she always did. Brigetta waited in the car. She had climbed into the front seat, and as soon as he turned the corner of Margaret's street, she leaned over. Hot breath, tongue in his ear, hands on his thigh, his crotch.

Surprised, delighted, he kept his eyes mostly on the road, but he used one hand as best as he could. By the time they pulled into the driveway, he had one of her breasts out and her skirt hiked up around her waist. They staggered into the living room, leaving pieces of clothing as they went. He felt dizzying energy, a pulse, all his senses wide open. She was aggressive and forceful, egging him on until he had her hair in his hands, his legs shaking against the sticky leather couch. He held her afterwards, and she leaned into him, sniffling. Did I hurt you, he asked, but she shook her head against his chest.

Brigetta ruffled his hair with her fingers before she walked upstairs. He heard the squeak of the shower, the cascade of water behind the walls. And for some reason, he remembered the paint on the shirt in the bathroom, the single drop on the tile. He hadn't been in the guest room again, having decided to let her have her surprise. She seemed to have settled on some sort of blue, which he thought would probably be nice. Like the ocean, the sky, all pleasant things.

———

LATER THAT NIGHT, Maddie called to tell him that while she'd been away, Margaret had a biopsy taken from her right breast. A tumor, small but benign, was removed afterwards. Grandma was here, Maddie said, but I can't believe Mom wouldn't have called me to come home. And Tony listened, thinking his daughter was becoming as dramatic as his ex-wife. Sounds like it wasn't a big deal, he told her, and eventually, Maddie calmed down. I'm really tired, she said. He told her he was, too.

By the time he turned off the lights and joined Brigetta upstairs in their king-sized bed, she was already snoring. She'd kicked the covers off and slept on her stomach, one long leg gleaming in the light from the hallway. One pink heel turned sideways, one triangle of purple silk covering her left buttock, and at the curve of her waist, a swipe of blue paint. He walked over to get a closer look, but when he approached the bed and bent over, it was gone.

In the bathroom, he splashed cold water on his face. He thought about calling his father the next day, he considered checking on his sister. Later, as plans and memories faded and blurred into sleep, he remembered the ferry ride back to London, the vastness of the cold, empty sea, and later, the starchy smell coming from his mother's clothes, boxed and stacked and waiting by the open door.

Fall

THE LAST SIGN was that evening, of course: Brigetta's final, inspired seduction. He didn't realize it at the time, didn't come home from retrieving his only child after her month of European exploits and think: this is the end. But it was, and it is.

The next morning, he'd gone to the office as usual. Brigetta slept soundly (he'd marveled about this later); her bright red hair was vivid against the white sheets. He wanted to wake her, to say goodbye (for the day, he thought), but he wanted to reward her, too, in a way. For the night before, for what he felt for sure what the beginning of a regeneration. Once Maddie gets settled at school, once the apartment building is finished, he thought, perhaps they'd take a trip over the holidays. New York, Miami, anywhere she wanted. Maybe he'd surprise her with southern France; she'd said she wanted to go. In this flush of goodwill, he let her sleep. He tiptoed around, even showered downstairs and bought his coffee at a drive-thru Starbucks on the way in. A busy day, and neither of them called the other. And when he got home that night, every trace of her was gone.

Oh, there were signs, he saw that now. The time she avoided him at that party, wouldn't dance "because it was too crowded." The way she looked beyond him sometimes when they were out. Her involvement with the destined-to-fail boutique. Even he knew you couldn't make rent in that neighborhood selling old clothing and crap. The takeout dinners. And there were bigger signs. Banner-sized, neon, glittering signs. When she moved her things out (so obvious!). The movies, the late nights, even the painting of the bedroom (his bedroom!).

She left a note. Basically: I'm sorry. I'm sure. Don't call. Some irritating reasoning about him spending the last few weeks before college with Maddie, without the distraction of her. Annoying assurances about his awesomeness (her word) and her unwavering regard. He spent a day pacing the house, kicking sand down by the water, speed-dialing her number again and again. The next day he drove down to the boutique.

He'd been there only once before, at the grand opening, which was really a dozen or so people gathered around a small table with a cake and plastic glasses of Cabernet. The owner, Charlene, thanked him for "loaning his girlfriend" and tried to make small talk about his work. Mostly, he evaded her. She was effusive about Brigetta's décor choices and business advice, and the two women kept darting into the back room for God-knows-what.

The muralist was there, although he didn't think about this until later. Leonard came in with another guy, both unshaven and lanky, the other guy wearing a corduroy jacket although it was still eighty degrees at nine o'clock. When he shook their hands, they smelled like cigarettes and something chemical. Leonard has a show coming up at a local gallery, Brigetta said, and he'd give a lecture on street murals. Both men had paint flecked into their long hair. Leonard's hair was curly, past the collar of his flannel shirt. Also a senseless choice for a summer night, Tony thought. They had paint on their hands, under their nails. Some white, a bit of yellow. Blue. Leonard had an unnerving way of looking at Brigetta until she looked down. Even this didn't raise a flag. The guy was strange; he was making them all nervous, Tony reasoned.

Afterwards, he drove her to the apartment building he had

designed. In the upwards flicker of the streetlights, the steel framing glittered like stars. He stood with his arm across her shoulders and told her about his plans. She asked a few questions, mostly about the corner units and how they'd be supported. It reminded her of the tall building in Chicago, she said, where you could stand on a glass platform and look down under your feet.

Sure, there were signs. But it wasn't until two days after she left, when he stood at the window of that ill-conceived store and saw her bright hair, bouncing on her back as she laughed and laughed, and the mousy Charlene hanging a dress on a nearby mannequin, and the muralist, this Leonard, laughing along with them, smoking a thin, girlish cigarette—then he realized the dye was cast. Neurons fired; connections were made.

The days went by. He took Maddie shopping for a microwave for her dorm. They bought a bedspread and a foldable wardrobe. She stayed over a couple of nights while Margaret was visiting her mother in Palm Springs. They made popcorn and watched movies. He overheard her on the phone one night, telling her friend she'd have to miss the party because she couldn't leave her dad alone. At the end of August, she left as planned, loaded her Toyota with bags and boxes and kissed him on her tiptoes. Tony drove back from Agoura Hills, sobbing like a child until he had to pull over and collect himself. He vowed to quit working so many hours, to get more sleep. It was busy at the firm. They were starting on a new proposal, a mixed-purpose building in Santa Monica. On the days he wasn't driving to the apartment building site, he spent long hours at the office.

Once, he convinced Brigetta to meet him for coffee at a place near the boutique. She came in after he did, her hair still wet at ten-thirty a.m. He felt a pang when he saw her. She ordered a caramel Frappuccino, her normal drink, but asked for extra whipped cream. He thought maybe she had put on a few pounds. He asked about business at the boutique; she asked about Maddie and Berkeley. Finally, he asked her to come back.

She was wearing a pair of jeans faded almost white, and some sort of shawl or vest, with bits of colorful fabric tied into knots at the bottom. The short, tight shirt she wore underneath ended at her ribcage, and he could see her bare abdomen, the smooth, flawless skin there.

"Anthony." She lowered her head a few degrees. "Surely, you saw this coming. I mean, was it really a surprise?"

He gripped the coffee mug with such force that the tips of his fingers burned. "Why didn't you tell me what was wrong? We could have fixed it—"

"You think I didn't?" She blinked, shaking her head. "It wasn't something I could tell you, like, Anthony, can you remember to put the dishes in the dishwasher, or please don't put your arm across my neck while I'm trying to sleep."

"I didn't know, I could have—"

"Are you listening? It's not those things, I said." She crossed her arms. "It's more complex."

He looked across the coffee shop, at the long line of customers. Most looked down at their phones. He was glad they'd made it in before the crowd.

Her brown eyes watched him. "I felt, I *feel* you aren't exactly mentally present most of the time. Aside from that, which is a problem, I don't think we really have much in common."

"What?" he said. "The age difference?"

"No, other differences."

He reached across the table and put his hand on her forearm.

She looked at him. "You're a nice guy, Anthony—"

"Oh, Jesus."

"What do you want me to say?" She pulled her arm away. "It was very lonely, living with you."

Tony leaned back in his chair, remembering similar conversations and pushing the memories back. "I wasn't the one who was always gone," he said. "It wasn't until you started hanging around that store, going to art lectures and pretending to be some sort of artist—"

Her eyebrows raised into two arches which he now noticed were dull brown in color. In the fluorescent lighting, she looked startlingly like her mother.

"Just say what it is, Brigetta." He picked up his phone from the table, put it into his pocket. "You met someone else, that's all it was."

"Anthony."

He pushed his chair back, and it barked along the wood floor, which was covered in scratches. Some cheap material, he thought, and then: I'll be goddamned if she's going to leave first.

"Anthony," she said again.

He stood up. "Have a great time with your muralist." His legs trembled. "Quite a lucrative career from what I understand."

Brigetta looked around the crowded room, tucking her hair behind one ear. "I'm not seeing him anymore."

"Then, is there—" He hated the pleading tone of his voice, so he stopped.

"Anthony, you never even told me about your mother. I mean, I knew she had died, but to think that after almost two years—"

He sat down, heavily. "I don't understand. You left because I never told you some sad story about my mother's death?"

"No, but so many things made more sense after that."

"You can't do this, Brigetta. You don't get to psychoanalyze me unless you want the same.

Her eyes widened.

"You're young, and you're flighty, and I should have realized sooner."

"Flighty?"

"You can't make up your mind, and you jump from one thing to another. You're twenty-eight years old, and don't have a real job."

She reached for her purse. "I'm going to go now."

"You think life is about lectures, and parties, and discovering yourself. Well, sure, for a while it is. But then you grow up. Look at you, dressed like some sort of hippie. What do they call it now, bohemian?"

"You can't talk to me like this." She stood up.

"No, don't go." His face was burning. "Stay, enjoy your coffee. You don't have anywhere to be, do you?" For a moment, he stood and looked down on her. She seemed small, shorter than he remembered. Her hair had faded to a carroty red color. And still, his insides churned. He could picture her at the beach house, legs pulled up on the leather couch, or naked and humming amidst the smooth surfaces of their lavish shower or resting on the deck with sunlight sparking her hair. "Don't go, Brigetta," he said again, and then he turned and walked out.

December

SOMETIMES HE SAT in the third, empty bedroom, starting at the mural. Let me paint a picture for you. Only it wasn't painted at all, only a charcoal outline of intent.

Maddie came home for Thanksgiving. She loved Berkeley, loved her teachers and classes and everything about the campus. They had dinner at a restaurant, before she and Margaret were to drive to Palm Springs for the rest of the week-end. He invited them to his place, offering to order a complete Thanksgiving dinner. Margaret had declined; she had always hated the house. She'd wanted to stay put, close to her job, close to Maddie's school. She hadn't understood why he needed the change. It was too run down, she'd said, too much work. But it had been more than that, an ocean more. He saw that now.

So they had a pleasant meal at a restaurant, turkey and everything else. And when Margaret went to the bathroom, Maddie told him she needed another biopsy. It would happen in December, and could he call to check on her? Maddie would be back for Christmas but wanted to make sure everything went okay. She was afraid.

The outline for the mural was a series of lines, not quite parallel, humping here and there like a mountain range or the lines on a hospital life monitor. He spent hours in his old, slip-covered recliner, working on drawings and looking up now and then, trying to decide what it was meant to be. He finally settled on a horizon, a half oval for the sun, zigzags below for mountains, or perhaps, waves. Without any color it was hard to tell. Brigetta had taken down the paint sample cards, and he couldn't find them anywhere. Also gone: the bag of paint supplies. She'd find a use for them someplace else, probably. All that remained were these several sketched lines, cutting the white walls into sections, hinting at their purpose.

The house whistled with wind. Even from upstairs, he could hear the white noise of the water. It was December, and probably too cold to have the walls open, but he didn't care. He wore a flannel shirt he'd felt silly for buying but now sported frequently around the house. He'd also treated himself to a new coffee machine, which brewed single cups in two minutes. It was a Sunday, but most of the morning he planned to work. Maybe he'd head out for a Christmas tree. Maddie would be home in ten days, and she'd promised to stay at his house for one week of her vacation.

Ensconced in the old, comfortable chair, he thought about

Margaret, her biopsy. He should call her, he realized. Also, when was the last time he called his dad?

A work acquaintance had invited him to a holiday party, a casual affair at his home. Tony thought about buying a new shirt. He'd have to go out soon to have enough time. Some of the office staff would be there, the attractive woman recently hired to manage the secretaries, some single friends of the man's wife.

He could shop for Maddie while he was out. Maybe the bookstore? What did she say her favorite class was? History? Psychology? He couldn't remember. Rising, he finished his French Roast and took a last look at the mural. Next week, he'd hire someone to paint over it. Maybe a pale beige, or he'd stick with the white. The room could be a place for him to relax. He'd get a couch, maybe some shelves. How many times can someone look at the horizon, anyway?

SMOKE

WHEN THE SMOKE began to seep under the closed door, Arma was sitting on one of the padded kitchen stools, her elbows on the granite island, its gleaming surface now sticky with blood. She took hits from a menthol cigarette and through her own diluted exhales watched the smoke from the bedroom; delicate, almost ethereal, it spread across the teak floor like some white, billowing rug. A beautiful rug, she thought, with mountains and valleys and swirling parts, pulsing, moving, expanding and contracting, like her lungs, now full of minty smoke, now empty. She shook herself from the deep thoughts, realized the codeine was probably to blame. She no longer felt throbbing in her feet, or the sting where the glass had cut her forearm.

In high school, Arma and her friends bought menthols by the case, pooled their resources and split the packs. She liked the scent, the cool blast as it entered her, the feminine lettering on the package. People said menthols would ruin your lungs faster than regular tobacco, but she and her friends were young and disbelieving of any danger beyond not getting what they wanted. She remembered that brave Arma. Arma of the short, denim skirt, its ragged edges and dangling strings brushing against her tanned thighs. Arma who walked through the night, any night, any place, without fear.

She stubbed out her second menthol on the granite, next to her car keys, which she'd been holding at the back door before she'd decided to come back, sit down, and think things over. Anybody who watched television at all knew that if a fire was small and contained behind a closed door, there was plenty of time to get out, to call somebody, to live.

The kitchen stool was one of three, chosen by Johnny quickly at a nondescript furniture store in the mall. Yet, when she had suggested they keep looking for something that better matched the modern look of the kitchen, he had defended his choice as though he'd spent months—no, *years*—contemplating the exact, perfect, fucking kitchen stools when he had, in fact, made a quick decision with no rationale, and like every conversation they had which turned quickly into an argument, Arma found herself confronting inexplicable and deep-seated distortions, rather than merely, practically discussing kitchen stools. And if she wasn't careful, the "discussion" would last and last, into the weekend and possibly weeks into the future, where it would be recast as "the time she didn't respect his choices," or "tried to control him," or "ridiculed him," and after a thorough wearing-down, she would soon begin to second-guess herself because maybe, just maybe, she *did* all those things, *was* all those things instead of a youngish wife stupid enough to think that for once, just once, they could talk about fucking kitchen stools and not whatever else was going on in his mind, that minefield she had no map for, no warning signs.

She tapped another cigarette from the pack and lit it. Gingerly, she stood and walked on the sides of her feet to the refrigerator, an appliance she irrationally anthropomorphized into a nurturing, substantial safe place. When things were at their worst, the fridge hummed along, making ice, keeping a steady temperature, holding sustenance. Often it was the only sound in the house, at night after he'd fallen asleep, those many nights of her desperate insomnia, her eyes as big as an owl's as she paced the rooms.

Shit, she thought, the codeine. She needed to keep a clear head. After she'd stepped on the glass, after she'd yelped in pain and fallen onto the carpet in the family room, cutting her arm on an especially long and jagged piece, after she'd bandaged everything as best she could with regular-size Band-Aids, after *that*, she'd found the leftover Tylenol with codeine prescribed for her broken wrist, the time she'd fallen while running, because she'd been hungover and tired and not seeing straight at all.

Opening the stainless-steel door, she retrieved a bottle of water from the fridge and drank half of it in a series of gulps.

Johnny hadn't been a smoker, not when she met him. He was tall and good-looking and always smelled good. Once, probably five years into their marriage, she read about pheromones in a magazine, and suddenly, she understood the way her knees buckled when she nuzzled into his neck, the insistence between her legs when his dark hair brushed her face. The attraction had lasted for quite a long time when everything else had burnt out.

Arma walked over to the couch, still holding the bottle of water and letting the ashes of the cigarette trail after her. She perched on the armrest. The couch had witnessed everything: naps, sex, meals, arguments; it had been her bed for months at a time, when she'd lie awake staring through the window at the moon, watercolor clouds, the backyard trees conversing in whispers. She always left the kitchen light on in case he startled her in the middle of the night; she slept with one arm over her ear, her face. She thought many, many nights about suitcases, and long drives, and hotels along the straightforward road that led south, where her mother still lived her best life in the condo by the beach. But Arma never left.

When she had started planning, she would imagine conversations with the judge, in the courtroom where she'd certainly end up. She'd tell him about the manic behavior, the ambushes, the cruelty. But was there physical abuse, the lawyer would ask. His lawyer. And she'd be forced to say no, although her body had certainly paid a price over these years. A tremor in her hands, weight loss, omnipresent shoulder knots.

The smoke was insistent now, creating a light fog that had reached the hallway. Arma limped to the kitchen, where her blood dotted the ceramic tile, smeared in places where she'd stepped in it already. She grabbed her keys, opened the door to the garage, and stepped down. Her car was nestled between steel shelves along one wall—where they kept the extra non-perishables Johnny liked to buy in bulk from Costco—and the other car, his Prius. His tendencies toward preparedness and prudence, once admirable, now seemed yet another product of tortured over-thinking. Everything had changed, absolutely everything. They were like two understudies thrust onto the stage, wandering amongst the same props that had always been there.

With two clicks, Arma opened the trunk of her car. Bending over, she pulled the green duffle bag into the light. Inside were the only items she'd allowed herself to pack: two changes of clothes, one nightgown, a bag of new, unopened toiletries, a small stack of childhood items, and the Ziploc with the syringe. She straightened up and closed the trunk. The bag had been in there for five months, another exercise of pretending, a crutch she relied on, trying to convince herself she'd really do it. This time.

Arma was thirty-two. She'd been married to Johnny for ten

years. They would be, anyway, if they made it to August. Which, certainly now, they would not.

The thing was, he was two people, her Johnny, and this was very hard to explain to people. Even after all this time, it was difficult for Arma to reconcile. He was still thoughtful Johnny, gentle and passive, trying to please her, trying to try. But that Johnny lived deep within the other one. Years had put layers and layers over him until only a faint spark could be seen, the merest reminder of his former ways. Even his posture had changed, the way he held his body. Everything strained, inward. Eyes perpetually squinted. He looked many years older than Arma now. Most of the time, she couldn't recognize him at all.

She went back into the house and blinked when she saw the smoke. Almost as if she'd forgotten about what had happened, about what was about to happen.

The first inkling, the first definite flare she could recall, had happened during a weekend trip to Vegas. They'd been married a couple of years by then. Johnny had started the job at the financial services company where he still worked; their dating phase had fishtailed with his completion of law school and a couple of years working long hours at a large firm. Arma was at the car dealership then, answering phones and helping in the showroom. Bethany was in the service department; sometimes, she and Arma took lunch together or went for happy hour. Three couples were going to Vegas, Bethany said. Cirque de Soleil one night and dancing the next. Did Arma and Johnny want to join?

It was just what they needed. Johnny was exhausted and stressed. He left at seven in the morning and often didn't get back until seven or eight in the evening, sometimes later. Arma convinced him to take Friday off, and they carpooled with Bethany and Mark, following the other two couples on the long drive from L.A. to the desert. She'd imagined days by the pool, rounds of frozen drinks blurring into more drinks before extravagant dinners. Long, leisurely mornings in bed with room service. And all of that happened. But what also happened was Saturday night, when Johnny completely flipped out on the dance floor at the club at Mandalay Bay, storming into the casino where he yelled at her, his face red and unrecognizable, his fists clenching and unclenching as Bethany, Mark, and the rest awkwardly stood by. Before she left, Bethany grabbed Arma's shoulder. "Will you be okay?" Her eyes huge and searching. And Arma had been embarrassed—can you imagine? Embarrassed! Of course, she'd told Bethany. This is so strange, she said, not him at all. She honestly thought maybe someone had slipped something into Johnny's drink, or perhaps a blood vessel had burst into his brain. She considered taking him to a hospital.

The next day: apologies, the strain of awkwardness thicker in the light of day. They lounged in the poolside cabana, and Arma did her best to steer the situation back to normal. Everyone tried. Now, years later, she had a long list of these occurrences, times when Johnny would turn from the person she knew into someone she didn't, startling episodes when his anger, his frustration, his imbalance, his emptiness (she tended to think of "it" as all of these things at one time or another), his *problem*, would rear its ugly head. She went through many phases, trying to manage it, employed countless strategies to make it better, avoid it, confront it. It fatigued her to think of all the ways she had tried to take responsibility onto herself. Even now, it was a hard habit to break. Although Johnny lay unconscious in the bedroom, she still felt some small ration of guilt for what had happened the night before: the broken things, his rage, even her own injuries.

The smoke was dense and insistent now, a real presence. Arma pulled her shirt up over her mouth and nose, walked across the room, and opened the sliding glass door. She stepped onto the patio in the backyard and filled her lungs with fresh air. They'd been in the house for seven years. Once Johnny had settled into his new job, a corporate gig with regular hours (and, she thought at the time, more manageable stress levels), they scrounged together the down payment for the three-bedroom ranch on a quiet street. Arma had never wanted children, so she imagined the spare bedroom filled with weekend guests, a chef's kitchen where she could try new recipes, the extra den where Johnny could watch sports. When she thought back to that time —shopping for furniture, working together on house projects, meals on the patio while the kitchen was being renovated—it was like another life.

She took one last look around. The lovely lemon trees at the corners of the small yard, the rose bushes lined up next to the house and finally, the ashtray overflowing with cigarette butts on the patio table. Everything soiled, she thought. Johnny had been a rare, casual smoker when they met— parties, occasional week-ends—but had taken it up in earnest a few years into the marriage. Another circumstance she didn't like but tried to live with, another thing that added a layer to the growing wedge between them.

For some reason, this one, smaller thing, the smoking and how much it disgusted her, ignited a fire in Arma. It all came flooding back: the moods, the blame, the way his *being* asserted itself over hers, like a shadow darkening an entire room, an entire life. Her life. The careful treading that had become her existence. The arguments about things that had not happened, about his convoluted visions of the world. The crushing weight of it, until she couldn't breathe.

She pulled her shirt back up over her mouth and nose and

pushed through the smoke. She'd do it. It wasn't what she'd intended, but maybe the universe had stepped in. She hadn't started the fire, but she certainly could look the other way while it burned. Finally, *she* would be first, what *she* wanted, what *she* felt.

In the garage, she grabbed four bottles of water from Johnny's Costco stash, threw them onto the passenger seat. Lifting the lid of the plastic trash bin, she dropped the pack of menthols inside. She checked her wallet for the bank cards she'd need to drain their checking account, to transfer the funds from their savings. She'd have to wait a while, of course, until the insurance company had done their best, until the wreckage was sifted through.

The garage door opened noiselessly, another appliance that soldiered on despite malfunctions everywhere else. When she reached the end of the street, Arma couldn't remember if she had closed it, so she circled back to make sure.

She passed the large house on the corner. There was a housewarming party when the family moved in. Wine, appetizers, the back, retractable door open to a view of the expansive lawn. Soon, the house, similar in size to theirs, was surrounded by scaffolding and construction trucks. Once finished, it was utterly transformed. A second story stretched the length of the ground floor, which had been expanded until it left no driveway at all. White and red brick covered the entire façade; the rest was dun-colored, with white trim and inexplicably—a true blue front door. This new, daunting structure served as a sentinel; it was the first house you'd see when you entered the neighborhood. During the holidays, they had the best lights and decorations. In spring, the walkway was planted with fresh blooms.

Arma let out her breath when the house was out of view. Soon, she passed the grocery store, Starbucks, Del Taco with its ancient, round, orange tables and metal umbrellas. Two old men sat outside, their food between them on spread paper. The car idled at a red light. She hadn't bothered to turn on the radio, but around her, the air buzzed. Her heart, pumping. The sun asserting its bold presence. She watched the men as they talked quietly. One reached for his burrito and held it with great care as he brought it to his mouth. Behind her, someone honked.

She turned, and a haze passed before the car. Fluttering, jumping, spreading and contracting. Gently, some bumped into the windshield, making the faintest thuds. Like fingers on a tabletop. The night before, Arma had been on the couch, watching the news. A short segment about the migration of billions of monarch butterflies. They traveled from Mexico to eastern Canada then back again, year after year. With lifespans of mere weeks, it could take four generations to make the trip. And she had pulled the soft blanket up to her chin, thinking about the journey of one, lone butterfly, his destination unclear but predestined, moving by instinct alone.

Another honk behind her, this one less polite. Slowly, Arma accelerated through the intersection, pulling over to the curb once she was through. She turned the engine off and looked through the windshield. It was less concentrated now, the nebulous but frantic movement, and she could make out the detail of one butterfly, then another—the flash of orange, tiny dots against a definite stripe of black and sometimes, two, upright antennae—as they floated around and above the car. Each making its dogged way forward, keeping distance from the rest but moving as a group, nonetheless.

She reached for her purse and found her cell phone inside. Her fingers were shaking as she tapped: phone, contacts, Johnny. A vision of his face, mutated, jaw clenched, hair standing in clumps made by raking hands. The sound of breaking glass. His rounded back as he stumbled toward the bedroom, spent. *I will never see that face again*, she whispered.

Outside in the warming air, the migrating butterflies persisted, and the phone continued its musical ringing. Pressing the cold edge against her ear, Arma leaned her head back and closed her eyes—only for a moment, she vowed—and waited for him to answer.

VERDANT PASTURES

The Lord is my shepherd; I shall not want.

— *PSALM 23, NEW AMERICAN BIBLE*
TRANSLATION

"I'M OKAY, I'm okay, I'm okay."

I hold the steering wheel for a few moments, close my eyes. The GPS dumped me in the middle of the small town of Rhododendron and from there, I followed Mr. Chance's directions. When I open my eyes, I'm looking at the house, my father's house.

Vines cover the left side. They grow from two mounds, entwining and thickening upward until the plants meet the roof and spread like cowlicks. The front of the house—a cottage, really—is beige and nondescript. A wooden porch has been added onto the square, main structure; four steep steps lead up to the house's above-ground entrance. The double door is white with French windows and appears to be new. It's the house's only flair.

I get out of the small rental car and look around. From all

sides, green, green nature presses in. Tall trees surround the house—some type of fir, I believe—and two have grown so close to the foundation, it's hard to determine which was there first, trees or house. One is cozied up right next to the porch and when I move a little closer, I see it's two trunks growing side by side, joined at the bottom.

From a distance, tires crunch down the only winding lane leading to the place. The roads around here are overgrown and mostly without markers, so Mr. Chance's emailed directions required attention not only to landmarks and geographical features, but to time and imagination too. "Drive for about ten minutes down this road," he wrote, "and look for a burned-out house." Or "You will see a creek and feel like maybe you'll drive right into it, but you won't." I know I'm at the right place because there's a blue pickup, covered with moss, just as he said there would be.

A gray sedan pulls behind my car, and a tall man unfolds himself from the front seat. He's blond and lanky, younger than I thought he'd be.

"Mrs. Dent?"

I nod and wait for his approach. His hand is thin and cool to the touch. He's probably in his early thirties. "Nice to meet you, Mr. Chance," I say.

"Please call me Richard," he says.

"I can do that. You can call me Mrs. Dent."

His eyes widen slightly.

"I'm joking. Charlene."

He laughs, much relieved. "Nice to meet you, Charlene." He holds a folder in his left hand, propped against his hip. All about my dear old dad, no doubt. "So," he says, "this is the house."

"Okay," I say.

Richard steps onto the first porch step and opens his folder. "Your father, Mr. Powers, bought this house in 1996 from a Mr.

Willard Dubree. He paid $26,000, cash." He climbs the remaining steps and fumbles in his pocket until he retrieves a key. "I don't know if you're familiar with this area, Charlene."

"I'm not," I tell him. Why would I be?

"Real estate in and around Rhododendron actually does very well, because of all the skiing nearby, and because of its location in the beautiful Mount Hood corridor." He turns the key in the lock and the door swings open. "This type of house, in this condition, if it were closer to the main roads, or any of the resorts, or the central section of town, well, it wouldn't be unreasonable to put it in the one hundred thousand range."

We step inside, where the air is still and woodsy. I look around the sparse room. The whole interior of the place seems to be in my sight, at this moment. A basic kitchen, a small living area with a couch, one recliner, a television on a stand, and a door that must lead to the bedroom. "Dollars?" I ask. "One hundred thousand dollars?" It seems like an unrealistic amount for such a small, basic place.

He nods. "Technically, it's a one bedroom but there's a loft." He points upward to a protruding platform holding a mattress and nightstand. Everything—the loft, the walls, the ceiling—is made of honey-colored wood. Richard gestures with his folder. "As I said, it *could* be listed for that amount if other circumstances were in our favor. There's another issue as well."

I walk over to the coffee table. Two copies of *Car and Driver,* a stack of newspapers, a book of poems by someone named Wendell Berry. A blue-tinted glass sits near the corner, one inch of some dark liquid remaining at the bottom. I think about the fact that someone could take a DNA sample from the edge of that glass and another from my saliva, and the two would match up. Here, in this cottage in the Oregon wilderness. Me, Charlene Dent, a dentist from Palmdale, California.

"I was saying, Mrs., um, Charlene. I was saying there's another issue that would hold up the sale of the house."

I turn to Richard, the local estate administrator who has managed to track me down. "What issue?"

He flips through his pages. "When your father bought the house from Mr. Willard Dubree, another loan originated at the same time. Mr. Dubree was making payments to his brother, Mr. Raymond Dubree, to purchase the land the house sits on. Apparently, one had inherited the land and the other, the house. However, the first Mr. Dubree never finished making payments and well, he died. This was in 2002."

What is he saying? My brother and I own a house but not the land under it? "Who owns the land then?" I ask.

Richard's mouth spreads into what he probably considers to be a rascally grin. "I've been researching that, and I believe it's going to be a Ms. Rochelle Dubree, daughter of Raymond, who lives in Massachusetts."

I pick up the glass from the coffee table and carry it over to the sink. I can smell the contents now, whiskey. From the kitchen window, I have a view of the other close-set fir tree. As I watch, a reddish bug darts around the trunk then disappears under a flap of bark.

"It will take some paperwork, but you may have to pay for the acre of land before you can sell it. I hope I'm not getting ahead of myself. Obviously, if you and your siblings decide to, you can keep the place.

I face Richard, who seems much taller inside the house. There is a high, V-shaped ceiling but even so, I feel confined. "We don't want his house," I say. "We don't want anything." The air has gone out of the place; my lungs tighten. "I haven't seen my father since I was ten years old, and I'm thirty-eight now, in case you were wondering."

He shakes his head.

"My father was a mechanic," I say. "He went to work one day and never returned. No phone calls, nothing. He had no family that we knew of, and nobody ever came looking for him. My mother has never remarried. I think a part of her always thought he might come back."

Richard looks at the worn brown carpet, too embarrassed to meet my gaze.

From this angle, I can see into the bedroom: a rumpled, green bedspread, two slippers pointed away from the bed, waiting for feet. I want to go back outside, take a deep breath. "Wait, did you say siblings? It's just me and my twin brother, Charles. He's Charles Powers, Jr., actually."

Richard reopens his folder, shuffles through the papers for several maddening moments. "I have that, yes. Charles Powers, Jr., of Apple Valley, California, Charlene Dent of Palmdale, California, and Melissa aka Missy Powers, of Sacramento, California."

I can hear it now, nature. Birds singing and calling, live things rustling through the trees. The fish of the sea, the birds of the sky, every creeping thing that creeps on the earth.

The estate administrator watches me. He waits.

"I don't know that person either," I tell him.

———

IN VERDANT PASTURES he gives me repose; Beside restful waters he leads me.

He refreshes my soul. He guides me in right paths for his name's sake.

I SIT on the porch of the house where my father lived for the last twenty years of his life and try to imagine Melissa aka Missy

Powers. My half-sister, apparently, who will arrive later this afternoon. One dilapidated chair sits next to the handrail that outlines the porch. I can see round stains in the wood where my father set his glass. I put my coffee mug right on top.

Last night, I slept in his house. The blossoming town of Rhododendron, apart from being miles from this place on its outskirts, also has, in terms of hotels, mostly ski resorts too rich for my blood. There are a couple of Best Westerns, but they are some distance away. After the trek to LAX, the flight to Portland, and the drive into the Oregon wilderness, I'd been exhausted. Richard volunteered to take me to the nearest market, where I picked up coffee, cereal, bread, peanut butter, fruit, and bottled water. He told me about his initial conversation with Melissa Powers. She'd been surprised, he said, but wanted to see the place. Just like me.

I had no exact plan when I came here. I had cleared my schedule for yesterday, a Friday, and figured whatever needed to be done, I could do over the long weekend. Monday is Labor Day, and my dental office is closed. Dent Dental—a funny name, I know—but I was half-way through dental school when I met Brad, and more-than-eager to shed "Powers."

There is still non-perishable food in the cupboards at my father's house, but the refrigerator has been cleaned out. I've discovered that my father liked all sorts of canned soup, mostly Minestrone and Italian Wedding, and he kept his dry goods— sugar, rice, oatmeal—in airtight containers or bags. Out here, he probably had run-ins with all sorts of critters. This was one of thoughts that kept me awake on his stiff sofa last night, that, along with all the rest.

I sit on his porch and look out into the woods. How many times had he relaxed here, like this? Richard told me much of his information about my father came from a Mr. John Stillwater, the owner of an auto shop in town. Apparently, they were friends. In early 1996, my father stopped in Rhododendron when his truck broke down and decided to stay. He asked around until he found this place to buy, which took all the money he had. Mr. Stillwater towed the truck here, and it never ran again. I'm planning to drive into town to speak to this man after I've finished my coffee.

I pull my cell phone from my pocket and dial my mom. I've already talked to Brad. Everything at the house is the same, he said, no messages from the agency. He's a patient man, my husband. The coverage here is surprisingly strong; Richard told me there's a tower nearby, hidden somewhere in the trees.

"Hello?"

"Mom, it's me."

"Charly, what time is it?"

"I don't know, nine-thirty? Mom, I'm at his house."

She says nothing.

"I'm wondering—and I hate to ask you—but the guy here says my father bought this place for twenty-something thousand dollars, cash. Does that sound right? Did he have that kind of money?" I wait for her to tell me he cleaned out their account when he left or stole from his job.

"I don't know," she says. "He didn't take anything from me, not that there was much to take."

My mom was a secretary at a car dealership back then. Throughout her whole life, she's worked a variety of secretarial jobs, until she retired three years ago. My brother and I never felt the lack of a father, not once. She put me through college somehow and gave my brother money to start his horse ranch. Recently, she bought the first brand new place she's ever lived in, a condo close to Brad and me in Palmdale.

"How are you doing with all this?" she asks.

"I'm okay," I tell her. "But it's like being in a stranger's house."

"You have some memories, don't you?"

"Yeah, of course," I say. "I remember the smell of engine oil on his hands. I remember that loud laugh he had. I remember going out to Apollo Park to fish."

"He was fun, wasn't he?"

That's what she remembers, after what he did? I picture her sitting on the patio at her own place, looking out at the manicured grounds. It makes me happy. "I'll call you later," I say.

I hang up and call Reverend Tran. I want to ask him about forgiveness, about what we do if we can't. He doesn't answer so I leave a message, asking him to keep me in his prayers.

On the way into town, I pass over a creek I don't remember on the drive in. It's beautiful, like something on a postcard. The bridge is wooden and painted dark red, and it stands out from the lush green like a signal. Underneath, bubbling, clear water rolls over mossy stones. It isn't difficult to see the appeal of this place, especially compared to the colorless desert where I live. Here, everything is blooming and green and alive; the trees tower and press in on all sides. It's the perfect place to get lost in.

A few hours later, I cross over the creek again on the way back to my father's house. It's mid-afternoon, and the light is entirely different now. The red of the bridge is faded; the creek is sluggish and dull. John Stillwater was not at his auto shop but his cousin, who wheeled himself out from under a car, promised to tell him I came by. I had lunch at the Zigzag Mountain Store and Cafe and wondered how often my father had been there. I spent some time wandering around, and lost track of time.

I find the house without trouble; already, the place is familiar. When I come around the last bend, I see a compact, red car parked in front. Someone is on the porch. The sun is coming through the trees in little bursts, and I can't make out the person until I've almost reached the steps. She stands above me on the porch, and for a long time, we stare at each other.

"Charlene?" she finally says.

"Melissa?"

She comes down the steps and stands in front of me. We are the exact same height. Our dark blonde hair is the same shade, although mine is cut short and hers falls past her shoulders. We have the same thin build, the same pronounced collarbone, the same freckles across our high cheekbones. She's like a younger version of myself and even though I'm a twin, I've never seen anyone with such a strong resemblance. My brother favors our mother and not until this very moment has it occurred to me that I must look something like Charles Powers, Sr. And so must Melissa Powers. Without a doubt, she looks like me.

"You can call me Missy," she says. "If you don't mind. Do you go by anything shorter?"

"No," I say. "We call my brother Junie, for Junior. It's something I said when I was little, and it just stuck."

"You're twins, right? Mr. Chance told me that."

"Right. Do you want to go inside?" I ask. I've been here less than twenty-four hours, and I'm already acting like I own the place.

We go into the living room and Missy accepts a glass of water. We sit down. She tells me about her life: twenty-six years old, veterinarian assistant, single. Her mother also lives in Sacramento, owns a design business and has been happily remarried for ten years. Her stepfather works at a bank, and Missy has a nine-year-old half-brother, Zachary. Our father left when she was six, and they never heard from him again. Just like he did to us. As we're talking, I notice a hesitancy in her, something hard to describe but easy to sense. It's in the way she says something and quickly looks down, or keeps shifting in her seat, arranging her clothes. I wonder if this comes from being abandoned, if people notice the same uncertainty in me. After some time, I get up to make tea, moving easily through my father's kitchen to find the teapot, cups, a plastic container of sugar. Outside, the patches of blue between leaves and branches are fading, losing color. An engine whines to a stop, and we both walk towards the front window to look.

A man steps out of a large, black truck. He's wearing a bandanna, folded like a headband, and a black tee shirt. He has a short, graying beard and a round belly, and he stands for a moment, looking over the house.

I open the door.

"Miss Powers?" he asks.

Missy steps around me.

"Wow," he says. "Am I seeing double?" He puts one foot onto the first step. "Which one of you is Charlene?"

"I am," I say. "But it's not Powers anymore."

"Excuse me," he says. "I'm John Stillwater. Your father was a good friend of mine."

He's much younger than my father was, but older than both of us. Fifties, if I had to guess. Once introductions have been made and we're sitting in the living room, he can't get over the fact that Missy and I are both here.

"So you didn't know about each other?" he asks.

"No," we assure him.

"And you had no idea where your dad was?"

"No," we say.

He closes his eyes, and we wait while he collects himself. When he opens them again, I notice they are kind eyes. Brown, doe-like eyes. I like him, I can't help myself. And at that moment, I trust him and whatever he's going to tell us.

"What can I say?" He looks around the room. "I spent so many hours here, hanging out with Charles. It may not feel that way to you, but to me, he was a great guy."

Next to me on the couch, Missy crosses her arms over her chest.

"He always talked about you kids like he was in touch with

you. I mean, I knew he hadn't seen any of you for a long time, but I had no idea—"

"How did he get around," I ask, "if his truck was never repaired?"

"Funny you should bring that up," he says. "I've been keeping your dad's motorcycle at the shop. It's out there in my pickup."

Are you kidding me? Add to the list of things I don't need: one motorcycle, one house in the middle of nowhere, one little sister.

"What can you tell us about how he died?" Missy asks.

John Stillwater looks at me.

"Mr. Chance told me the circumstances," I say. "But I'd like to hear it from you."

He sighs, hangs his head. "There's a place where Charles liked to go. The bike will only take you so far, then you hike for a mile or so. At the top of a summit, there's a flat rock where people like to picnic. A little way beyond that, a creek with the freshest water you'll ever see, trout the length of your forearm."

"He liked to fish?" I ask.

He nods. "They found him near the creek. Heart attack, the coroner said. That was four months ago now."

There are so many places my father loved: this house, Oregon, that creek. So many things he loved more than his children: fishing, cars, being alone. I stand up. "How far is the creek, did you say?"

"I can take you there," he says, "but it's too late today. Tomorrow's Sunday. Shop's closed."

Missy clears her throat but still sounds hoarse. "I'd like to see it."

John stands up and shoves his big hands into his pockets. "I'll come back in the morning. There's something else I don't know if that estate guy told you girls."

I flinch at being called a girl but decide to let it pass. Annoyingly, it feels comforting, like he's going to take care of us. At the same time, my inner feminist recoils at this thought.

"Your dad was cremated," he says, "and I've been storing the urn until I could figure out what to do with it."

"Is that in the truck too?" I ask.

He tilts his head, trying to figure me out. "No, but I'll bring it with me tomorrow." His legs crack and creak as he walks toward the door. "I think there's nothing Charles would have liked better than to be dumped in that creek."

"Jesus," I say.

"Goodnight," John says, and he closes the door behind him.

———

Even though I walk in the dark valley I fear no evil; for you are at my side
   With your rod and your staff that give me courage.

When I wake up on Sunday, Missy is quietly puttering around the kitchen. I smell coffee and watch as she drops bread into the toaster.

"Sorry," she says. "Did I wake you?"

"No," I lie. Sitting up, I crane my neck to see into the bedroom. For some reason, I still can't bring myself to step in there, but Missy had no trouble sleeping in his bed. She'd found an extra set of sheets and matter-of-factly, had carried the others to the stackable washer and dryer behind a door off the kitchen. I'd fallen asleep to the hum and creak of the washing machine.

"Do you take cream and sugar?" she asks now.

"Both," I say.

She brings me a cup and sets it on the low table next to the poetry book. "It's so quiet here at night. And dark. I'm used to streetlights and cars, people passing by."

"Do you live with your mom?"

"Oh, no." She sits on the recliner across from me, pulls her feet up. She's wearing a flannel shirt over a tank top and black leggings. Her hair has been brushed, and she has a bit of eye makeup on.

Most days, even when I'm working, I don't get around to putting on makeup and I keep my hair short, one length, so I can easily comb it and tuck it behind my ears. That helps when you're leaning over patients all day.

"I have my own apartment," she says. "My mom, Larry, and Zach live close by."

"He's nice, your stepdad?"

She nods. "I was sixteen already when they married, so he's not like a dad to me, not really."

"I wish my mom would have found someone," I say. "She's one of those people who's content being alone most of the time. She worked until a few years ago, and she keeps busy with church, her book club. But still."

"I wonder if our mothers are similar," Missy says.

My cell phone vibrates on the table. I pick it up, excuse myself, and take it and the coffee to the porch.

"Hello?"

"Charlene, so nice to hear your voice."

My eyes fill up—I don't know why. "Reverend Tran, it's nice to hear your voice, too."

"You dear one. We missed you and Bradley at the Italian dinner. I got in late, extremely late for an old man like me. I didn't want to disturb you."

"How was the spaghetti this year, Reverend?"

"Much better, much better." He chuckles softly. "But you asked me about forgiveness, Charlene, and I know you are going through this terrible time, losing your father. Let me read something."

I hear pages turning, and I take a deep breath, waiting.

"'Peter asked the Lord, how often will my brother sin against me, and I forgive him? As many as seven times? Jesus said to him I do not say to you seven times, but seventy times seven.'"

"That's quite a lot," I say.

"Yes, Charlene. Seventy times seven. You will find that the path of forgiveness is easier to walk, however, and we all have a long way to go."

I picture Reverend Tran, short legs propped on an ottoman, tan face wrinkling around the eyes. At eighty-three, he is lithe and sprightly. I know I'm being childish, but I ask anyway. "But what if someone doesn't deserve forgiveness? Doesn't ask for it?"

He thinks about this for a moment. "Are the best gifts always the ones we ask for? Remember, Charlene, you have one father, who is in heaven. He will help you."

"I'm okay," I tell him. "Thank you so much for calling me back."

"You're welcome," he says. "You have so many blessings around the corner. Have you heard anything about the baby, your baby?"

"Not yet, Reverend. We're waiting for a phone call."

"God bless you, Charlene, and safe travels back home. You are missed."

I hang up and sit in my father's chair. The coffee is still hot, and Missy has added the perfect amount of cream and sugar. I watch as John Stillwater's truck rumbles over a fallen tree segment, branches crunching underneath the enormous tires, and comes to rest behind my diminutive rental car. I take a deep breath and get up to meet him.

An hour later, the three of us linger on the porch. While I quickly showered, Missy and John chatted animatedly in the kitchen, their tone entirely too festive, all considering. Was I the only one who wasn't feeling happy about going to see where my father died? When I came out, dressed in the only pair of jeans I'd brought and a short-sleeved shirt, he sent me back in for a sweatshirt. Now we walk, single file, to his truck. He lowers the tailgate so Missy can add a Diet Coke and a candy bar to the cooler he has packed with sandwiches, bottled water, and apples. He closes the tailgate with a loud click.

"Why didn't he ever fix his truck?" Missy asks, and we follow her gaze to my father's moss-covered pickup, its tires sunk into the loamy grassland, still as a watercolor next to the wall of tangled vines.

"Or have it taken away?" I add. Truly, I have seen the way tasks can go undone. Adults allow years to pass before they venture into a dentist's office. One man explained to me a complicated procedure of stuffing homemade putty into a hole in one his molars before every meal. The pain would come and go, he said, but often woke him at night. For years he went on like this, and so, it seems like a small thing to let a broken vehicle grow moss.

John rubs the fringe of his beard, looking at the truck. "To be honest," he says, "I think it reminded him of the past. He never said such a thing, but that's the impression I got. It was a, what do you call it—"

"A token," Missy says.

He considers this and nods. It's as though it wasn't the word he wanted but is close enough. "As long as that truck wasn't moving, neither was he."

We climb into the cab of John's truck. Missy sits in the middle but angles her legs into the open space next to me. Reaching for seat belts, we chuckle when we almost bump foreheads. And then we're off.

The countryside around my father's house is deep green on

multiple levels: the canopy of trees blotting out the sun, the low-hanging leaves dense as green nets thrown over the branches, the vegetation covering any sign of path or clearing. We view it all from our elevated position; John's truck is high and powerful. We traverse the red bridge, and the wooden arch comes alarmingly close to the truck's cab. Below, the creek is clear and fast.

"Your dad loved that truck," John says. "I'm not sure how to explain it. He wouldn't let himself have it."

"Maybe it was too expensive to fix?" Missy says.

He has one hand on his thigh; the other arm is propped on the steering wheel, his right hand dangling over the top. "Naw," he said. "He could afford it."

"How did he get his money?" Missy asks. "He couldn't have been very old when he moved here, probably his forties?"

"Forty-five," I say, because I've already done the math. They both glance over at me.

"He helped me at the shop once in a while," he says. "Your dad was talented with cars, I can tell you. He also had some other income, although I can't speak to that."

"What do you mean, like Social Security or something?" I ask.

"He was too young," Missy says. "Until recently, anyway."

"Welfare, then?" I say. "Disability?"

"I don't know," John Stillwater says.

He pulls the truck into a cleared section at the side of the road and continues driving through high grass and around a line of trees. Missy and I bounce in our seats as we travel over the uneven terrain. It is wild and overgrown and yet, faint traces of prior visitors are visible: a broken branch, heavy with leaves, hanging like an injured wing; twin tire grooves pressed into the grass here and there. John Stillwater parks the truck next to a white-trunked giant. Someone has carved a heart and "12-6" in the bark; inside the heart are initials, but they've become unreadable over time.

I get out of the truck and tie my sweatshirt around my waist. Amidst the dense trees, it's much cooler than it was on the porch of my father's house. September's average temperature during the day is around seventy degrees and the average rainfall for this month is 1.01 inches. The elevation is 1776 feet. All facts I looked up online after Mr. Chance called me.

I had been sitting at the kitchen counter in the late afternoon, looking through the paperwork from the agency again. At night, I'd lie awake thinking we'd read it wrong; there must be some form still to finish, some procedure we'd done incorrectly. But every time I opened the folder, the same words were still there: Application Complete. After seven years of trying for a baby, I couldn't get my head around the fact that there was nothing left for Brad and I to try, nothing left for us to do. The agency was averaging six to eight months from application completion to assignment, and we were at the seven-month mark.

The cooler John Stillwater packed is canvas and has a long strap, which he puts over his head and onto one shoulder. He's wearing a baseball cap pulled down close to his bushy eyebrows. "It's about a mile on uneven ground," he says. "Watch your step and stay close. At the end, there's a climb, but you girls will do fine."

Missy looks at me and crosses her eyes, as if to say: What does he know about us?

We head straight into the woods—at least, that's how it seems. But then I notice it, the faintest, narrowest path, like a pencil line drawn onto the green. It's wide enough for one foot, so it's like walking on a tightrope. Of course, we don't walk that way; our feet crunch and smash the plants on either side. Overhead, some bird calls to another.

"Was he very fit, then?" Missy asks. "I mean, if he made this hike regularly?"

John slows down but doesn't stop walking. "For a man of sixty-five, he was in great shape. Strong legs, big man. He helped me lift an engine once from an old Chevelle. He did all the maintenance in and outside of his house, and he shoveled snow for a couple of his elderly neighbors every winter, along with his own. He'd get up on the roof to clear it, even after I told him I'd do it. Stubborn man, but strong as an ox. Only his heart was weak, I guess."

Missy walks beside me, her blonde hair swinging. "My mom told me he'd spend all day on the weekends fishing for trout on the Sacramento River and come home with nothing."

"Why?" I ask, but even as the word leaves my mouth, I remember.

"Always threw them back," John Stillwater says. "Every damn time."

I feel a surge then, a tightening. My father's hands, threading a hook down the length of a worm, my father's hands, gentle around a fish's heaving belly as he dislodges the same hook. Sunlight reflecting from the scales of the fish as it flies over the water. I keep walking, one foot in front of the other. John Stillwater's back is broad, blocking any possible view of what's ahead. Missy has fallen behind me in this dense section; on both sides, my arms graze plant life as we walk. I blink steadily, remembering. My brother, Junie, pulling a worm from the Styrofoam container and letting it twist and struggle on his palm. My father strutting in his overalls, and Junie holding his stomach, laughing, laughing.

My breaths come faster. There is pain in an unfamiliar region, like aches from a phantom limb; something vise-like rises in me and grips my heart from inside. Missy runs into me; I have stopped walking.

She laughs. "Sorry."

I stand there, breathing, pushing thoughts away, getting oriented. "I'm okay, I'm okay," I whisper.

"What?" Missy says.

John faces us, one finger pressed to his lips.

We straighten and obey. Missy stands next to me. I can feel her presence as though she's a mountain, a house. We are several feet away from a clearing.

He moves to the side, and we can see beyond him to where a mother deer leans over, eating grass, next to a smaller deer, her mirrored copy, her twin, her baby. The day pauses. Insects buzz and click; birds flap and whistle. Something shakes the branch of a tree, and the mother deer startles. She looks all around, steps in front of the smaller deer and continues pulling grass from the ground. We watch for a long time, this lingering, suspended moment, and I understand how one day can be a thousand years, and a thousand years like one day to God. The mother is sleek and beautiful, with perfectly symmetrical ears and white fur on her neck and belly the same shade as the baby deer's spots.

A branch cracks underfoot. Suddenly, Missy leans against me so quickly that I stumble a little. I grab her elbow to steady her, and when she has righted herself and brushed back the veil of hair covering her face, I see that she is crying.

———

YOU SPREAD *the table before me in the sight of my foes;*
  You anoint my head with oil; my cup overflows.

WE SIT, cross-legged, on the wool blanket John has pulled from his pack. He has unpacked, also, the sandwiches and bottled water; the apples are wet with condensation. The sandwiches are thin slices of ham with mild, white cheese. It makes me smile to picture him making them in his bachelor's kitchen. The large, flat rock is already warm from the late-morning sun; through the blanket I can feel it.

The hike to the rock has taken almost an hour. The terrain grew increasingly craggy and steep. We kept a slower pace, mostly because of Missy, who doesn't seem to have much stamina. We stopped twice so she could relieve herself; she blamed the morning coffee. John has headed off now for the same reason, having finished his own sandwich. He told us we are about two-thirds of the way to the creek where my father died. This spot is perfect for picnicking, except that tiny spiders continue to scale the edges of the blanket and scurry towards us.

Missy swats one as she holds her sandwich aloft. She has pulled her hair into a ponytail, and her forehead glistens with sweat. We sit cross-legged on the rock, eating. Her bare ankles intersect under the rolled cuff of her jeans, and I notice a small tattoo of two Chinese symbols above her left ankle bone.

"What's your tattoo say?" I ask her.

"Hm?" She looks at it, still holding her sandwich delicately between her thumb and forefinger. "Loyalty," she says, "and strength."

One of the symbols is much more complicated than the other, and I wonder which is which.

"Do you have any tattoos?" she asks.

"No, not me." I stretch my legs out. My backside is going numb, sitting here. "My brother has an eagle on his back. He's sort of a cowboy."

"You said he has a horse ranch?" Missy says. "I've never been on a horse. Well, once I rode a pony at the fair, but I don't think that counts."

"Junie used to always invite us out to ride, but I've never

really liked it. I don't feel like I have control over what the horse will do. I don't like that feeling."

"Why didn't your brother come up here with you?" She pops the remainder of the sandwich into her mouth.

I lean back on my hands, considering how to answer. "He's very angry," I say, "even after all this time. He says he's not interested in anything having to do with our father."

She nods, chewing.

"My brother has two kids," I say. "My niece and my nephew. They're ten and seven. When they came along, for the first time I got a real idea of what it meant to be a father. Junie's great at it, somehow a natural. But I think that having them has made him even angrier at what our father did, leaving us like that."

"And you're not angry?"

"No," I say. "I don't know why. Are you?"

"Yes." She crumples up the plastic bag that held their food. "Mostly, I'm hurt. But on good days, I'm angry."

We hear a cough in the distance and turn to watch as John Stillwater emerges from the trees. His face is flushed red, either from sun or effort. It occurs to me that he may be older than I originally thought.

Missy pats a section of blanket next to her. "Plenty of room up here," she says.

"I've got to stand for a while," he tells her. "Stretch my old back."

He reaches his hands toward the sky, then out to both sides. His fingers are trembling a little.

"I wanted to ask you something," I say.

He squints up at me, waiting.

"Why is there an extra bed at the house, in the loft? Did my father have a roommate?"

John Stillwater turns around, looks through the tangle of trees we've just hiked through. Thick with green, buzzing with life, the land slopes gradually downward; above, sheltering branches and underfoot, shifting, crumbling rock that used to be mountain itself, to the spot where—although we can't see it from here—his truck is nestled in the high, high grass. He turns back towards us. "Most of my life, I've had a drinking problem. Ended up losing my house, my wife. Thank God we didn't have any kids." He looks down. "Charles let me stay with him until I sobered up. Drove me to AA meetings every night, took me to the doctor. Eleven years now."

For a few breaths, we listen to the buzz and breeze around us.

"Once in a while," John says, "Steven comes to visit. He stays up there."

"Who's that?" I ask.

He seems to have realized some error—a flash across his face —then resigns himself. "Your dad had a girlfriend in Portland before he ended up in Rhododendron. Steven is her son. He helped raise him for a while, and they kept in touch."

Missy rises onto her knees. "He had another kid?"

He holds his hands out, spread. "No, no. Steven was about two when Charles met him."

"Oh, for God's sake." Portland, another checkpoint on my father's checkered journey north. I stand up, my ears ringing. "He was a saint, I suppose. Nursed you back to health, took care of this kid *who wasn't even his*." I pick up the crumpled trash and begin to climb down from the rock. It's getting warmer, my legs are stiff, I'm losing my patience. "Forgive me," I say. "I don't want to hear any more. I'd like to get this over with so I can get back to civilization and call my husband."

"I'm sorry, girls," John says. "I don't know what to say. His story, what he was to me, what he told me, it's the only part I know."

Missy ambles down the rock after me, and we stand,

together, facing him. "Thank you," she says. "I appreciate you taking the time to bring us here."

He glances at me. "Charles didn't talk about it much, but I got the feeling he had a tough time growing up. Foster care, stuff like that."

Missy's face softens.

"I can't explain what would make a man do something like this. I don't have kids, so—"

"You don't need children to have an opinion," I say. "None of us have kids, right?"

His eyebrows come together, making a deep dent in his forehead.

I look him in the eye. "There's a Bible passage that always speaks to me. 'In the wilderness where you saw how the Lord your God carried you, just as a man carries his son, until you came to this place,' etc. There's no explanation, it's obvious. A man carries his son, a father takes care of his children. I don't need to hear about his upbringing. I don't need to psychoanalyze him, to understand him, to hear that he cared about me. It's too late."

Missy nods slightly, and it feels like encouragement.

"Maybe there's a simple explanation," I say. "He didn't want to pay the money, he was selfish, or he was able to put all of it out of his mind and go fishing, day in and day out. It's not for us to figure out or judge. There's someone else who will do that."

"Amen," John Stillwater says.

Missy shoves her hands into her pockets and kicks a rock across the clearing. She looks about six years old when she does this.

"Let's go," I say. "Let's see where Saint Charles liked to catch his trout and grant them their freedom."

We wait for John. Slowly, a grin spreads across his face. "I know you don't want to hear it, Charlene, but you remind me of him. You really do."

I roll my eyes, and Missy laughs.

"Let me get that blanket," he says. He walks past us and although Missy and I are looking around, wondering which way we'll go and noticing, now, the trappings of this natural place, the flutters and the fresh smells and the squirrel who scampers in a nearby tree; from the corner of my eye, I see when it starts to happen. John loses his footing on the coarse edge of the picnicking rock; his right foot sails out from under him, and as I turn, extending my hands as though from this distance I can help him, he crashes against the edge with a loud, cracking sound and falls to the ground below.

———

ONLY GOODNESS and kindness follow me all the days of my life;
And I shall dwell in the house of the Lord for years to come.

THE TRUCK KEYS jingle in my pocket as I tramp through the woods. Missy has stayed back with John Stillwater, who has broken something in his leg or hip and can't stand. They have two bottles of water, the candy bar, and the Diet Coke. From the small, cross-body purse she brought for the hike, Missy pulled out a prescription bottle with a couple of Vicodin left, and a baggie holding two joints. They decided on the marijuana, and as I began my hike back down the mountain, the sweet smell trailed after me for a while. John seemed to be in a fair amount of pain; the reddish tone of his face had paled, and he spoke through gritted teeth.

"Will you know which way to go?" Missy asked, looking me

up and down as though assessing my competence or checking that I wasn't, also, somehow hurt.

"Follow the narrow path until you come to the place where we saw the deer." John closed his eyes until a wave passed. "Then you're going to veer a bit to the left. South. Look at the sun. That's west now."

I've never been a Girl Scout or much of an outdoors person. I wish fervently that Junie was here, or even Brad, who sells insurance but knows a thing or two about camping.

"When you get closer to the road, you should get your cell phone reception back," John said. "Call the shop and tell my cousin where we are. He'll take care of it." He leaned his head back onto the blanket, which Missy had folded into a pillow for him.

"Try to hurry," she said, reaching out to grasp my hand before I left.

I feel a strange obligation to both, these people I didn't know before yesterday. This man who was my father's closest friend, this young woman who shares my blood. Such a dramatic expression—sharing blood—really, there's much more to DNA than that. And in another way, not much to it at all.

My thoughts are jumbling together, and my heart is pounding. I check the location of the sun and push through the trees, as individual as people themselves; none of them are familiar now. I think about Brad and our cozy bedroom back home, the way the bright sun filters through the blinds in contrasted stripes. In a flash, I remember jumping on my parents' bed with Junie, while my father ran around the perimeter, swatting at us with his white tee shirt. I remember burrowing underneath the covers and inhaling my parents' scents.

I've reached the clearing and recognize the spot where the mother deer and baby had been. The scene moved Missy to tears; some time ago, it may have affected me as well. Am I foolish to feel the motherless phase of my life has passed? Pride goeth before a fall and yet, is it a sort of pride to feel this way? Maybe, just maybe, some imbalance will be corrected. Those long years of toiling with Brad, the unfulfilled wish— was this what made my father's actions completely incomprehensible? Junie and Rosa hadn't tried nearly as hard and yet, they cherish their children. To try so hard for something that held no value for my father, to strive for something he squandered, not just once, but twice. There will never be answers; I'm at peace with that. I've been at peace with it for a long time, I realize. I keep walking, pushing through branches, kicking through vegetation. Suddenly, I'm missing the clear desert vistas, the crystalline, unencumbered night sky. My mom, Junie. Brad.

I keep a photo of Jesus, framed in the hallway at home. I have a habit of touching it whenever I walk by. In it, he's the shepherd Jesus: white robe, calm and loving expression, eyes that seem to follow you everywhere. He is constant, I know. I keep putting one foot in front of the other, mumbling an incoherent prayer as I go. He doesn't care if it makes sense; He always knows what I mean.

My steps fall into a rhythm, and I relax. The afternoon air is cooling, and shadows soften into blurry smears. After some time, I pause, wondering if I'm going the right way. I look around and keep going, and soon, a beam of sunlight fights through and catches the fender of John Stillwater's black truck. In my haste to manage the last stretch, I trip for a moment over my own feet and catch myself before I fall. Then I'm standing next to the truck, reaching into my front pocket for the keys, when a succession of rings, blips, and vibrations emanates from my back pocket. My phone, coming back to life. My throat aches. I wish I had brought one of the water bottles with me. Why hadn't we thought of that? I'd been too busy worrying about Missy and

John Stillwater, who were probably quite comfortably stoned by now, lounging beside that miserable rock.

I pull the phone from my pocket. Four missed calls, three from Brad and one from my mom. A steady stream of texts, also from Brad, but the final one catches my eye first:

Honey, there's news. Where are you?

I scan the rest, more of the same:

The agency called, call me!

Where are you?

Honey, please call as soon as you can.

I am so thirsty. I lean against the truck, take a deep breath. *I've called you by name*, I think. *You are mine.*

I press the numbers to call John's shop. I hope he's not in pain; no one should have to be. I've no idea how they will get that man off this mountain. Soon, I'll call Brad to see what he has to say and by tomorrow, God willing, I'll be back home where I belong. Can it be true? After all this time, has the agency matched us? How could I hope for this blessing, me, of all who deserve? I will rise to it, that's for certain. I'll do what should have been done for me. *Seventy times seven.* And if Missy or anybody else wants to come back later and dump our father's ashes in that forsaken creek, I'll have no part of it. I've already done my duty; surely, anyone can see that.

DEAR REBECCA

THAT DAY, that dress. Do you remember what you said to me in the vestibule of the First United Methodist, when I rushed out for one final, nervous bathroom visit, and there you were encased in a white crinoline like some duchess from another time? It was your grandmother's dress. You'd had it cleaned and cut loose in the bodice because you were much fuller than she had been. The skirt, multi-layered and multi-faceted, with lace and ribbon and what-have-you. In the square of September sunshine, you stood still, suffering the adjustments your sister made to your hair, your veil. She held the bouquet of daisies in her mouth—I'll always remember that—your tomboy sister with her legs splayed, trying to insert a pin where a strand had fallen. And you looked up, Rebecca, your green eyes like pieces of incarnate sea in that Midwestern church; you noticed me and tilted your head, ever so slightly. "Now you've done it," you said. Eyes twinkling, hands moving to the peak of that mountainous skirt.

Later, I helped you unclasp the garment, waited patiently while you struggled with the tiny hooks and eyes sewed in an impossibly close row as though your grandmother herself intended to keep me out, watched while you unbuttoned the delicate pearls that traced your breastbone, until I couldn't wait any longer.

The splash of color across your salty throat, the scent of clean linen that followed you from childhood, the proud mushroom of your abdomen. Inside, our daughter, still vague and unreal as the future itself. Against the cornflower blue sheets, your ankles nestled together perfectly.

From a fairly young age, your mother had entrusted you with the laundry. A dubious honor, considering the work involved and the size of your family. From time to time, my mother would announce the arrival of another Winstock baby with a disapproving voice. Now I see there may have been a tinge of jealousy involved. You told me about the Winstocks that didn't live—four in all—along with your memories of the ones that did. Your six brothers, your two sisters. The last, a pudgy girl with blonde ringlets and a soft mind. I wonder if you know, Rebecca, that Delia lived with your parents until they passed. But you needn't worry. Your brother Roger took her in, and they fill a gap for each other. Two spinsters but never alone now.

My childhood home was sedate and orderly, especially in comparison to yours. When I tired of those dark rooms and the gentle hum of the radio, which my mother often left on after the programming had finished, I'd kick through the tall grass and head towards your place. Over the barren spots and past the dilapidated barn with its splitting, curling planks, downhill to where the land failed into a secret creek, then back up the crest to where you were.

Shirts and trousers and each wrinkled sock, shook out and pinned in lopsided rows. Your mother's patchwork housedress, girls' bloomers and faded pinafores. Seeing you there, wooden clothespins clasped to your skirt and your eyes squinted in concentration, shaking a piece of cloth, and droplets caught the sunlight, was like experiencing art. At the time, I didn't fully realize the power of the image. You were my playmates' sister, aloof and bossy, but I couldn't join in when they teased you, not really.

"Here comes the little parson," you'd say, and I'd look down at my clean, buttoned shirt. You'd ask me what I was reading that day, and I'd tell you, because your interest was genuine. Sometimes we'd swap books, although they were harder to come by for you.

Our house was owned by the Shandleys. Our benefactors, my mother would say. Their land abutted your father's, both men continuing a family legacy. The Shandleys had farmed at one time but had continued cultivating only the orchards. Apples, peaches, pears. Apricots, which were trickier. The orchards did so well that they moved to town, had a big house built where the millstone factory used to be. But you know all of this, Rebecca. You know how I envied your house, your life. Your father worked hard, but the land was his; your family was loud and boisterous and always doing something.

I was proud of my father—I don't mean to imply that I wasn't. He worked hard in his own way. He studied and prayed and worried. Every Sunday after service, he'd come straight home and take a nap. That's how much it took out of him, leading that flock. Such an eloquence, people would say, such an easy air. But they didn't see what went into it before, what was drained from him after.

I sometimes drive into town and walk around on days when I'm up to it. The bustle and activity make me think of you. Coming in with your bonnet askew, face flushed, your basket full of whatever you'd managed to find. Those three rooms, the cozy bedroom and closet of a bathroom, the kitchen only big enough for one person. Sometimes I'd go in for a glass of water when you were cooking just so I could brush against you. But you were wise to me, you were always wise to me. I can't think of many happier times than the few years in that rented home, those three rooms above the widowed Mrs. Cranston. Your idea, moving to town and away from our families. My days at the clerk's office followed by blissful nights, the three of us together on the mattress my mother shyly offered as a wedding gift. Joanna's pink face as she slept in her own woven bed, before she grew too big for it. The time she got croup, and we bumped around for days and nights, sleepless and frightened, united in our care for her.

She's wonderful, our daughter. Many times I've marveled at her resemblance to you. She looks nothing like you, on the surface, nothing like either of us. Where'd that red hair come from, people would ask, grinning, and you'd always say you had a ginger great uncle. Uncle Mars, you'd say, and we'd hold our straight faces until later, when we could laugh about the red planet. It's that curiosity, Rebecca, that's one of the ways Joanna is like you. She wants to know about things, always has. It may be true that parents sometimes build up their children or over-look their faults, but I can honestly say that Joanna has never caused me a moment of grief, and hardly ever a worry. As a child, she was obedient and helpful. No problems at school, pleasant at home, an ideal sister once her two brothers came along. The worst I can say about her is that she's stubborn but then, I never saw it as a fault in you either.

I don't write poems anymore, Rebecca. I don't write anything, really. I keep a journal, and I hope someday, one of the children may want to have a look. Remember when my first poem was to be published, and we spent a week's salary on a dinner out, that extravagant wine? I sometimes wonder if losing your encouragement was the reason I stopped, or whether I was ever meant for it. Everything in my life is divided into two sections: before and after you. And it's too much to blame you for all the things I should have done or could have done, or to imagine where I may have been now if you hadn't died that summer when Joanna was only three years old. Three years old, Rebecca. How could you?

The leaves changed some time ago and now lie in tufts beneath trees or they swirl and lift like brief exclamations. As I said, I walk in town, but I stroll around the land here, too. Some distance from the cattle pens and the modern buildings, there is a clearing where a cabin still stands, hewn logs atop a concrete foundation. This is where Pauline's grandfather lived when he started the ranch. I like to go there and see his humble beginnings. The passage of time, the connection of family, the persistence of this land—it's all there. I suppose I'm like many old men with too much time on our hands, looking backwards as the future fades. Pauline calls them my "ramblings," which seems appropriate even if the word is a bit off. Going for a rambling, she'll ask me. She's a remarkable woman, Rebecca. Early on, our lives never intersected because Pauline's mother schooled all her children at home. I met her by chance, at a wedding, and Joanna was seven when we married. They are remarkably close. I know this fact wouldn't bother you, Rebecca, because your practicality always trumped whatever feelings you might have had yourself. Pauline found it curious that we never talked about what happened—you and I—once Joanna was born. We had that in common, I told her. What was there to talk about when there was a baby to feed and love? She wanted to know whether you'd been scarred by it, whether you'd been upset. But Joanna was ours in the only way that ever mattered, and if you remained violated by how you came about her, you never expressed or showed that to me in any way. And that's another testament to your strength, and something I think about every single day.

It may be possible that I've built you up to something you weren't, Rebecca. You were a headstrong farm girl who wanted to see Paris someday. We lived in town because you were tired of the country. You were fun and pretty and smart, always reading something, always encouraging me to do the same. You thought I could be a great poet when I was a town clerk. We had an occasional quarrel, but neither of us had the patience for it, too eager we were for each other's body and mind. I've had over forty good years with my wife, Pauline. She has given me two sons, a life of mostly ease, and her loyal and reliable devotion. I love her dearly, but never more than I loved you, Rebecca, and for this I feel guilt and resignation and if I'm honest, some measure of pain.

Joanna lives in town. She's never married, but it's not an unhappy fact. She loves a woman named Irene, and they've been together a long time. Joanna works at the bank, and she and Irene have traveled to many of the places you wanted to see. They have a lovely cottage-style home, and at last count, three dogs. They continuously take in strays, which strikes me as something you would have done. Pauline has been busy planning a dinner party for Joanna's fiftieth birthday. We'll have it here at the ranch, which is ours now. I take care of the business side of things, as I've done since we were married. We tried living in town for a while, but Pauline missed the proximity to her parents, her father especially. He's buried out here, Rebecca, in that clearing I mentioned. The family's first homestead. There's a tiny cemetery behind the log house. Pauline's mother and father are there, her aunt and uncle, her oldest brother, and one of her nephews who died as a teenager. There are two spaces reserved for us, and that's what I wanted to tell you. After all these years, I owe it to Pauline, and I'm so, so sorry, Rebecca. You, in town under that willow tree as you wanted, with the space alongside the fence for me. I can't do it, Rebecca, and it troubles me more than you might imagine.

That evening you came to me. Your collar torn, your face

puffy from crying. You had no chance, you said, and I believed you. I always believed you, not that you ever asked. Walking home from your friend's house after an afternoon baking cookies. The details of a tragedy couldn't have been more compelling if imagined. A young woman, still living at home but primed to break away. A day of innocence shattered by a strange man lurking in the shadows. And what was I doing during that time, at that crucial crossroads? Still living at home also, thinking about university, working at the clerk's office because my father got me the job, reading Russian novels and taking you to the weekend picture show. Spinning wheels, until the wheels came off when you were attacked. But I can't regret it, that's the conundrum. That attack, that vicious man, he pushed us both out of our stupor. I wanted you, but I'd been complacent and afraid. And hesitant, as I've been my whole life.

That day, that dress. My father at the lectern. Your mother sniffling into the handkerchief you'd pressed. Joanna's birth. Our feet cold under the quilt. You peeling apples for a pie as I press against you. Your soft hair, your gusty laugh. Joanna's tiny hands and later, her straight back the day of her graduation. Fiery red hair still defiantly displayed. And I can't help it, my two little boys, their dark features so like mine, their mother's thick eyebrows. Pauline's comforting hands. And my own mother, emaciated as you had been, her feet bent in such a way I knew she'd never walk away from that bed. The buzz of the thin, determined creek linking our childhoods. All of it, Rebecca. You're in all of it.

I saw your parents from time to time, of course. They were good to Joanna, but it became difficult for her, for them. They retained kindness towards each other but diminished as family over time. Two of your brothers and Delia live nearby, but the rest have moved away.

It's possible I blame you for too much, Rebecca. Your illness, your belief in me, your absence. You've become the never-ending question of my life and in many ways, the unsubstantiated answer. If Rebecca had lived, I think, I would have stayed in town and become a magistrate. Traveled the world. Wrote more of those awful poems, only they would have been good if you said so. Instead, I moved to Pauline's family ranch as she wanted. I can't decide if it was what I wanted, too, and this weakness is, in the end, the thing I blame you for the most. Because if you had lived, I would have become more resolute. Wouldn't I have? Your self-assurance would have bled over, would have seeped into me. I'm sure of it.

I'm infinitely sorry I couldn't protect you, Rebecca, that I couldn't keep one terrible thing away from you. And you've never stopped giving. You left me with this wonderful daughter who doesn't ask for anything or complain about her circumstances. And it makes me angry sometimes, how perfect you are and how I can never, never be as good. But then that's me, blaming you for everything all over again.

Every now and then when I'm able, I walk by the Shandleys' old mansion, now fallen into disrepair. The farmhouse on his property, where we lived when I was young, suffers the same fate. Shandley sold the orchards and retired someplace south. My parents are gone, your parents. The town, after all these years, is much the same. Expanded, but the main street remains. Mrs. Cranston's is now a bed and breakfast. I've often thought about renting our room upstairs but have never done it.

I wish I could lie with you, Rebecca, beneath that old willow, and divide my attention as I've grown accustomed to doing. I wish I could see you once more in those golden rays of light, hanging the day's laundry at the rise of the hill. Sometimes, in the way Joanna tilts her head or laughs with abandon, there you suddenly are. You would have loved her with a fierce and fixed passion, of that I'm certain.

That day, that white dress and the burst of life inside. That's how you'll stay, Rebecca. A young woman starting something she won't be allowed to finish, a spark that burned brightly and lingers afterwards, pulsing and pulsing, whenever I close my eyes.

Your Lucas.

THE LOVE OF YOUR LIFE SHOW

"WHAT THE HELL, JUNIOR?" Julie climbed into the car and glared.

"Juju, breathe."

"I said two-thirty!"

Junior closed his black-lined eyes to demonstrate calm. "They won't start without you."

She watched as he opened his eyes and grinned, crooked teeth gleaming, coffee-colored eyes like a dog that won't leave. She sighed. Her little brother. Four years since he'd shown up on her doorstep, after their mom passed and before he'd found his passion in life, which was—is—home decor.

They'd been scrolling Pinterest when the call came. "Is this Julie Renate Sandoval?" a voice asked, and her thoughts went immediately to St. Theresa's Parochial, where they'd always used full names. The nuns had loved Junior; behind their backs he called them *The Monochrome Despots*.

"This is *The Love of Your Life*," the man said. "We'd like to put you on."

"Oh," Julie said.

"You're aware of the application submitted by your coworker, Jeannie Mackeroy?"

And she remembered: a bottle of wine after work, Jeannie's cajoling, Junior's jokes. Her brother said her best shot at happiness was serial monogamy, each chapter ending with a bubble bath and a new hairstyle. Jeannie told him they couldn't all be queens.

The studio building was a gray, featureless box. Junior dropped her backstage. He waved his fingers and turned, the purple kimono jacket flourishing.

Julie followed a scurrying assistant down a long hallway. The set was huge, carpeted, kidney-bean-shaped.

"How are you, Julie?" asked the host, Lance Corazon. His eyes were beautiful and strangely unkind.

"All right," she mumbled.

He twirled her around. "Audience, are you ready to help Julie find The Love of Her Life?"

"Yes!" they shouted.

To Julie, they were all gleaming eyes and cavernous mouths.

Lance beamed. "Julie, you'll be placed in The Chastity Room. Finalists have been chosen by our computer, based on compatibility scores, DNA testing, and input from your friends and family."

She followed him to an enclosed, soundproof room. Inside, she sat uncomfortably on a plump, red couch. When the doors opened, the set was gone and sawdust stretched before her. She squinted in the half-light until she realized it was a brewpub.

"Over here," a man on a barstool called.

Randy was a computer technician who liked to ride mechanical bulls. He had thinning blonde hair and colorless lips. Quickly, they covered the basics over mugs of untouched beer.

"Where are the cameras?" she asked.

"You can't see them."

"Wow," she said. "This is awkward."

Suddenly, a voice boomed: *Please refrain from such comments. During the simulated date, avoid mentioning the simulation.*

"Sorry," she whispered.

Randy shrugged.

Again, the voice: *We'd like to interject a Conversation Starter, based on relevant information from your dating past.*

Randy scooted to the edge of his seat. Julie wasn't sure if he was The Love of Her Life. Maybe at first everyone found The Love of Their Life reminiscent of a flaccid sea creature.

Your Conversation Starter comes from Julie's high school boyfriend, Brad Kanwin. Brad says Julie was awkward in social situations, often making inappropriate sounds or jokes.

She snorted. She remembered Brad, of course. Junior called him *Big Top PeeWee* because of his large head and small penis, although she'd been unnecessarily cruel to speak of it, perhaps.

"The last I heard of Brad Kanwin," she said to Randy, "his hand fell off and he went blind." She laughed alone, wondering if the joke was inappropriate.

Wordlessly, Randy pressed the red button underneath the bar.

Her second date wore a Minecraft tee shirt and couldn't stop cracking his knuckles, even when she stared pointedly at his hands. Julie used her 50 Ways to Leave Your Lover pass to end their simulated fondue restaurant date. Maybe she'd be finished in time to catch *American Idol* with Junior, she thought, as her date's chair—with him in it—dropped into an opening in the floor.

Date number three. At the bottom of a flight of stairs, Reuben Straverskey stood near a gondola on a gurgling canal.

"Reuben—what the hell?"

"I didn't know it was *you*," he said.

Julie had been lusting after Reuben for months; only Jeannie knew. They all worked at the same bank.

With a push from the gondolier, they were on their way. Again, the cameras were somehow out of sight.

"So, did they find those checks on Friday?" she asked.

Reuben licked his fingertips and smoothed his eyebrows, a peculiar and regular habit that only now struck her as completely ridiculous. "Naw," he said. "Gunderson was beyond lunacy, the drama king."

She shifted her weight, and the boat dipped. "Is it weird, being here?"

"I don't know."

The voice: *Please refrain from talking about your reactions to being on the show.*

"I thought you had a girlfriend," she whispered.

Please refrain from whispering.

They rode in silence. Julie thought: If I were watching this episode, I'd turn it off. And she suddenly realized that Reuben was too goofy to be dated, that her lusting comments to Jeannie only helped pass time at work and that Reuben, although hysterical behind the bank counter, wasn't as stimulating on a simulated canal. Besides, what hilarious nickname would Junior call him? Even after their deadbeat dad bolted for parts unknown, even when their mom turned sick, bitter, and tired, Junior always made her laugh. Julie pushed the red button protruding from the side of the boat. A giant hook appeared and picked Reuben up by his belt. His legs kicked comically as he floated away; the audience laughed with gusto. Julie put two fingers in the corners of her mouth and whistled.

When the gondola hit shore at *The Love of Your Life*, Lance helped her out. Julie wondered how long she'd been drifting. Overhead, a screen flashed details from her life: Favorite Movie – *Clueless*; High School Music Choice – Alternative; Career Aspiration – Head Teller. At the top, one word blinked continuously: UNMATCHABLE.

Julie stepped down from the giant carpeted kidney and saw him immediately. Tall and handsome, a mouth full of uneven but white teeth, bright eyes shining out from all that black.

"Junior," she said. "You're still here."

PAR AVION

Peter

HIS MOTHER'S condo still smelled like paint. She'd been moved in a little over two months, having finally sold the house in Bellflower where he and his sister had grown up. Pearl, his sister, had picked up a brochure about the place: "Emerald Villas, an affordable, independent-living senior community." For almost a year, their mother had been on the waiting list for a two-bedroom unit; finally, in April, a Villas rep had called with hearty congratulations—as if it were some final destination lottery—and she'd been settled by June. And now, mid-August, the place seemed much smaller than Peter had remembered, stuffier and more confined and certainly, much darker with the windows covered.

He crossed the small living room and pulled back the curtain. Outside, manicured green accentuated by patches of flora, smooth walkways with benches situated along the way. He let the curtain drop and turned around. Dust billowed lazily in the late afternoon haze. The light brought out the gleam of the marbled tile and the nap in the beige carpet. Both were new.

Buyers could choose from a small range of neutral colors and materials: fresh paint, up-to-date flooring, a new skin for the rooms. His mother had kept the comfortable blue sofa and the sharp-edged coffee table that had given his youngest, Ryan, three stitches when he was a toddler. In fact, his mother hadn't bought anything for her new home, and the worn furnishings made it seem familiar to Peter in some confused, fun-house-mirror way, like a pared-down, slightly crowded version of the old house.

In the kitchen, he opened the refrigerator. A jug of unopened orange juice, six bottled waters, condiments in the plastic shelves. He closed the door, and a puff of frigid air ruffled his hair. The kitchen was small but plenty for one person; his mother had never been much of a cook. Moving her in had gone mostly without a hitch. At some point, they'd have to contend with the small storage unit in Bellflower, crammed with things she couldn't let go but didn't need. Pearl lived in Cerritos, which is why they'd focused the search here. Peter was further away in Long Beach, where he'd opened his law office after his oldest son, Reese, was born. Reese was eleven now; they'd been there over ten years, he realized.

He walked into his mother's bedroom, which was also dark, with the shades closed over the only window. He turned on the light. The bed was made, the dresser uncluttered, nothing out of place. To be fair, this was how it would look whether his mother was here or not; she'd always been a very neat housekeeper. Even after parties, when the house had been crowded with friends or relatives for an entire day or evening, he would wake up to find everything tidied up. To this day, the sound of clanking dishes was a soothing one; his mother must have stayed up late, all those times, putting everything right while he was falling asleep.

Pearl had called Peter that morning, her voice bordering on

frantic. He'd had to cancel a ten o'clock meeting and a lunch date with his wife. It was something the counselor had suggested, a weekly lunch to "touch bases away from the house." They took turns choosing a location. Tanya usually picked a restaurant close to home, even though she didn't work, and he was the one who had to drive over. That day, they'd been planning to meet at a deli near the law office, his choice. But then Pearl had called and although she said she'd been to the house twice already, Peter had decided to come himself.

She was a warm person, his younger sister, and certainly she took much of the responsibility for their mother, but Pearl lacked common sense. She'd talked to their mother Sunday night, she said, and had been unable to reach her since. It was Wednesday now. Peter couldn't help thinking there could be something Pearl had forgotten or overlooked.

He went back through the living room and opened the closet in the foyer, where Pearl said his mother's suitcases should be. Empty, save for some jackets and a few small boxes. He went back outside and circled the block to confirm there was no sign of her car. What else he was supposed to do, he didn't know. They'd both been calling (straight to voice mail) and texting (no response) all morning. Pearl had spoken to a couple of their mother's friends; no one had any idea where she was. There was nothing written on the calendar in the kitchen, something they'd been conditioned to check from their school days, when their mother color-coded activities and wrote reminders and encouragements: Final Day of Swim Team!, Pearl's Piano Lesson, or, Happy Birthday!!! She had always done this, even before the divorce from their father; afterwards, when it was the three of them, and especially when Peter and Pearl started driving on their own and becoming more independent, she gave them many freedoms but always stressed the importance of saying where they'd be, what time they'd return. And now here *she* was, missing, without a word to anyone.

Peter stood on the small patch of grass next to the front door. It was midday, summer in southern California. He could feel where his moistened tee shirt clung to his lower back. Should he talk to a neighbor? Should they call the police? Really, he had no idea. She was a grown woman, after all, sixty-two years old. He knew he should be worried and yet, as he scrolled through emails and missed calls, as he remembered his two o'clock meeting and the pile of paperwork on his desk, even as he went back into the warm, dark condo where everything was stubbornly orderly, Peter felt mostly annoyed at his mother, and in general, quite put out.

———

Anita

WHEN SHE OPENED HER EYES, they were traveling over a bridge. On either side, white cables flashed by, cutting the sky into geometric bursts of color. She peered through the taxi window, catching a glimpse of expansive, blue-green water before the car was back on land. She must have dozed off.

Anita didn't remember the impressive bridge, but it did bring another memory: nighttime, a line of yellow lamps, a much smaller bridge lowering and separating, disappearing under the road on either side. A procession of boats passing through. A salty kiss. A white button-up shirt that was softer than it looked, the warm skin underneath.

She cleared her throat. "The bridge, is it new?"

The driver looked at her in the rearview mirror. His thick, black eyebrows tilted together. "No. It has been there always."

He was probably twenty-five years old, and it had been forty-two since Anita had been to the island of Euboea, in Greece. The *only* other time that summer when she was twenty and had come—much like this time—on some crazy, insistent impulse.

On the island, trees lined the road. Soon, they were making their way through residential areas, the streets filled with businesses, shops, and people. The city of Chalcis was a mix of incredibly old and modern. One moment, they drove under an arch made of ancient brick; the next, sleek, white apartment buildings lined up, shoulder to shoulder. Anita asked the driver to take her near the shore and after some back-and-forth about time and cost, he agreed.

She had booked a fairly expensive room in a tourist section, where the island came closest to the mainland, separated by a narrow strait. Opening her purse, she took out a packet of envelopes, held together with a rubber band, and a folded, Google map, on which she had marked the return address from the envelopes. The hotel was less than a half mile from that mark. Another memory surfaced: eating some sort of pie, crusty bread wrapped in foil, cheese melted and steaming inside, standing by sparkling water, always by water, hands entwined.

The driver pulled next to a curb and looked at her expectantly.

"This is it?" she asked.

He nodded, opened his door.

She got out and peered up at what she realized was the backside of the hotel. Four stories with a service floor underneath, the rectangular building was simple, classic, and painted white. This is how Anita remembered the country: sunny days, white buildings, and blue sea, bursting tastes and smells, warm breezes.

From the start, this trip had been vastly different. She had been able to purchase a first-class ticket, for one. Selling the house and buying the condo had provided her with a decent chunk of money and after investing most of it, she'd decided to splurge. It was something she'd rarely done, while raising children and worrying about setting aside for her older years. Well, here she was, older.

When she reached her room on the third floor, she propped her suitcase in the corner, used the restroom, and then pulled back the heavy curtain. Her mouth fell open at the sight. Mountains loomed in the distance, framing a hillside of haphazard, white architecture. The only thing in common between the varying sizes and shapes of buildings was that each one was crammed with windows. And why not? Shimmering water, dotted with white-sailed boats, spread like a rug before her. Directly below the hotel, a wide colonnade, lively with pedestrians, hugged the shore.

She went to the bed and sat down, retrieving again from her purse the packet of letters. Each one was almost identical: pale blue with a border of bold red and darker blue slashes. Another flash of blue: the stamp that read "Par Avion" and under that "By Air Mail." She flipped through, looking at the colorful variety of stamps. Some were classical figures in white; others showed buildings or modern people she couldn't identify. All the stamps included the words ΕΛΛΑΣ-HELLAS, which she'd always assumed was "Greece;" she could find out tomorrow, when she went to buy a travel guide.

Anita had been a bookish child, although most children she knew growing up were more bookish than kids today seemed to be. Her grandsons were eleven and nine and constantly attached to *devices* (their mother's word). Anita had kept a bookshelf stacked with picture books she'd read to them after their bath, and longer stories recommended at the bookstore. She still had most of the books but kept them in a closet at the new place; the boys hadn't asked for them in some time. In fact, they didn't visit much anymore, always busy with soccer and baseball, music lessons and Boy Scouts.

She leaned back against the pillow and pressed one of the letters against her lips. She'd like to explain to her grandsons what it felt like to open the mailbox and see a thin, blue envelope with your name on the front, to know that a foreign boy had pushed his pen against the thin paper, licked the gummy flap, and sent it on its journey across oceans and countless miles. The rush of possibility, the exquisite anticipation. But her grandsons would laugh at that, especially practical, serious Reese, who had helped set up her email account when she moved to the condo. He was brash and sharp as a tack, her oldest grandson, and at eleven, he already had the rigid posture of his grandfather. At times, the same lack of focus. These boys, who could click on their phone or pad or whatever, and read any type of information, see absolutely anything they wanted to see—no, they wouldn't understand the heightened anticipation of a letter from a pen pal in Greece.

It had been Anita's mother's idea. In a children's magazine, she'd found an address where you could write to be matched with a pen pal. Even as Anita had penned that first letter, giving her age, grade in school, and address, a part of her didn't think anything would happen. Within a few weeks, she got a postcard with the name and address of a boy who was fifteen, living in Chalcis, Euboea, Greece. The boy, Costas Christodoulou, was a year older than her and his first letter was polite and factual: where he lived with his parents and older sister, what his school was like. She had read that first missive over and over, enamored with his formal English and the stylistic flair of his handwriting. They wrote about hobbies and friends, vacations and studies and eventually, they exchanged photos. Costas was tall and thin, with dark, curly hair. He wore sandals and leaned against a white, stucco wall, his face nearly covered by dark sunglasses. Their correspondence continued for six years, through adolescence and into young adulthood. They began to write more intimately. Costas had a girlfriend for two years; Anita dated a few boys throughout high school. At times, their letters took on a flirtatious tone. They wrote about their plans and frustrations. Costas's father expected him to continue his schooling on the island, but he had other ideas. There were arguments and threats but, in the end, he stayed and did what was expected. At the time, Anita's mother wanted her to enroll in classes at junior college, but Anita wanted to take some time off. It was 1975, and she was (she supposed now) doing most of the things that come to mind when anyone thinks of that decade. Experimenting, exploring. She had a job at the roller rink, spraying deodorant into skates and cleaning after hours, and a band of friends her mother called the Hippie Brigade. Things grew more and more tense at home and yet, Anita couldn't afford to move out. She felt unsure, trapped.

Outside the hotel, the sun was sliding behind the mountains. Anita got up and stood again at the window. The water in the bay was smooth as glass. She put the letters in the top drawer of the hotel desk and grabbed her purse. At the airport, she'd exchanged several hundred dollars for Euros. She probably could have gotten a better exchange rate at her bank, but the trip had happened so suddenly. Within three days, she had decided and bought her ticket, had packed her bag and closed up the new condo. The world through the window of the taxi on that early, summer morning had seemed vivid, and new, and promising. She had texted her daughter, Pearl, from the airport, only moments before she boarded. Anita hadn't told her children about the trip for good reason. They'd think she shouldn't, or couldn't, or wouldn't. But here she was.

She applied some lipstick and left the hotel room without looking back, determined to find something breaded with cheese inside, to inhale the fishy breeze off the water, and to buy a few colorful postcards to send her grandsons, who just might appreciate something that had traveled halfway across the world, after all.

———

Pearl

PEARL'S HANDS were shaking when she put the carafe back into the coffee maker; the thin glass rattled against the sides before settling into place. Too much, she thought. I've had too much.

She'd been up since four a.m. She had texted her mother several more times, had called and listened to the strange ringing that went on and on. Eventually, she resumed her normal morning routine: coffee, food, and talk radio. At her dinette, she stared over an empty mug at the messy kitchen. Time to go, she said out loud. A missing mother was no reason to skip work, even if the mother was over the age of sixty, which really wasn't considered old anymore, was it? Besides, *her* mother looked great for her age. Slim, with hair still the golden blonde of her younger days and kept in a wavy bob. Anita had always been what Pearl would consider a neat dresser, but recently she'd seemed to up the flair factor of her wardrobe: here, a bright scarf, there, dark denim jeans with metallic embroidery on the back pockets. She'd surprised Pearl at Christmas by showing up to midnight Mass in a new, caramel-colored leather coat, fringe hanging from the sleeves.

Where are you, Pearl whispered, checking her phone again. It was Friday morning. She hadn't heard from her mother since Sunday. Peter had been to the condo for the past two days, but she couldn't stand going there anymore. The last time, she had an honest-to-God chest pain, standing there next to the dining room table. She had to sit down and lean her face on its smooth, cool surface. It was the same table they'd had growing up, and she knew without looking that underneath one end, her name had been carved jaggedly into the wood with one of the good steak knives. Her mother had never found out and why would she? It was only when they'd gone over to supervise the movers and help their mother with the items she considered too valuable to trust to a licensed moving business that Pearl had thought about the carving and wondered if finally, she'd be found out. Would her mother yell at the thirty-five-year-old Pearl for the offence of her twelve-year-old self? She never found out. The table was transported without incident, her secret protected.

Pearl worked at a nonprofit agency that provided all types of assistance for the homeless. Job training and housing, referrals to shelters, hospitals, internet cafes, and places where you could get a free shower. Pearl's official title was Outreach Coordinator, but what she really did was brainstorm ways to get people and businesses to help with their mission. Maybe, for example, she could persuade a restaurant owner to offer incentives to its customers for contributing meals for those in need. She visited charity sales to stockpile blankets and jackets, and if she were convincing enough, she'd get them for free. A recent victory had been securing the sponsorship of a local hotel. They'd promised to develop an employment and housing package to take on several new hires. Sometimes, Pearl had the chance to work directly with the homeless people who came in, but only when they were short-handed in the office. She preferred working at the broader, more removed level; her heart wasn't strong enough to hear so many stories of lost family and diminished hope.

In the car, Pearl set her purse down in the passenger seat and leaned her head back. Her stomach was making dramatic sounds. She'd had a bland meal, toast and a boiled egg; it

couldn't be that. She pressed her hand to her forehead and found it cool but clammy. The coffee, she thought, too much. Mom, where are you?

She'd called her father the night before, which was probably what had gotten her out of sorts more than anything else. It was a long shot, of course. He rarely spoke to her mother and only whenever they were forced together for a family event, usually something for her nephews. When was the last time she'd seen him? Ryan's first communion the year before, she remembered. He and Jenny had come out from Idaho, where he lived in a big log house on a lake, like some sort of outdoorsman when he'd grown up here in California, in Gardena. Jenny had worn a big, flowered skirt and looked downright ungainly next to Pearl's mother, who'd been chic in a cream-colored suit. Oh, she was being mean. Who cared what either of them wore?

Pearl started the car and rolled the window down several inches. It was already hot at seven-thirty in the morning. Sometimes she could almost understand why he had left the incessant sunshine, the endless litany of warm days.

What would you like me to do, her father had asked on the phone. Emphasis on the *me*, not on the *do*. I don't know, she had stammered. She'd never made demands of him, wouldn't know where to start. He had moved away when she was thirteen, after the protracted divorce and a few trips back to clear out the garage, where her mother had been storing the accumulating boxes of his belongings. Sometimes, Pearl would peel back the tape and look inside, would run her hands over the spines of books, the sad jumble of socks.

Let me know when you find something out, her father had said. And she could picture him, hanging up the phone without a care in the world, sauntering back to the wide windows where he could gaze at his postcard-worthy view. In the distance, Jenny strolling through a field of wildflowers in that long skirt. Or doing something else equally nauseating. Pearl knew she shouldn't feel this way—it wasn't kind or really, very mature—but she allowed herself these petty thoughts from time to time, and it didn't hurt anybody, did it, so long as she didn't act on them?

On Del Amo Boulevard, a car had pulled off the road, apparently in a hurry because it was parked diagonally, its tail end jutting into the farthest lane. This caused a massive delay, of course, and by the time Pearl drew up near the vehicle, her heart was racing, and her back was stuck fast to the leather seat. She imagined her mother, passed out somewhere in her missing car, windows rolled up, trapped in the heat.

When she finalized her own divorce, Pearl had finally gained some insight into the events of her childhood, the strain her mother must have felt. At first, it seemed uncanny that Pearl had married someone so entirely like her father—distracted, selfish—and that he, too, had left to be with someone else. But Pearl's marriage had lasted only thirteen months, while her parents were together for almost twenty years, and Andy had left her for a man instead of another woman. The feelings of abandonment, disbelief, and insecurity, she assumed, were the same. She found herself divorced at twenty-four, just three years after she had dropped out of law school. Another sharp turn in the road of her life. Her mother had always told them not to marry too young (the implication being: don't do what *I* did), and Pearl waited for an "I told you so" that thankfully, never came. In fact, her mother had never said anything about Pearl's divorce, other than offering an ear and at times, a check.

Once, her brother Peter said he'd never met someone with a downward employment trajectory like Pearl's. Every job you get, he said, pays less and less. This wasn't entirely true, and yet, she couldn't really defend against it. She'd gone from the possibility of attorney pay to a job as a legal clerk, to a variety of jobs outside the legal field: credit union, animal shelter, the nonprofit that organized charity runs (they'd gone out of business, but she'd loved that job), Catholic Charities, the YMCA, and finally, her current employer. I need a job that means something, she had told Peter. She couldn't imagine working any other way. Lately, she'd been thinking a law degree would have come in handy. She could help a homeless person petition the court or provide representation for minor offenses. But she'd never admit that to Peter, who had stayed in law school and now had his lovely, two-story house and stunning wife, his great kids and new cars every few years.

As her car edged down the street, Pearl noticed that the stalled vehicle was steaming. There was a fire truck and a black smudge on the concrete underneath. It had been aflame, she realized. The smell was still in the air: oily, damp, acrid. Her stomach turned.

Where *was* her mother? She wouldn't have left without letting them know, without letting Pearl know. This was her mother, the most organized person she knew. The one who'd held her hand when she went to court to end her marriage. Her mother, who'd had no one to hold hers. A gurgling rose in Pearl's throat. What if something had happened to her mother?

Blinking the sweat from her eyes, she made it past the emergency vehicles and pulled her car to the side of the road. She fumbled with the door handle, opened it, and hurried around the front of the car. Clawing at her face to get her sunglasses off, she nearly tripped over the curb before she vomited right there in front of the Dollar Tree store, onto the neatly trimmed strip of grass and barely missing her new purple suede flats with the shiny, embroidered, gold sunbursts.

———

Anita

SHE STOOD at the base of the fortress, looking at the greenery draped over the top of the dusty, crumbling stone, at the places where it grew right through breaches in the wall. This ancient site was the top tourist stop in Chalcis, and Anita had spent the better part of the morning, first on the tour bus that brought them up the winding road then wandering through the cool rooms inside, looking at the artefacts and salvaged reliefs: lions with humanistic faces, horse-like creatures with beaks and long tails, others with wings or crowns.

Outside, it was hot and dusty. She thumbed through her guidebook, reviewing the main highlights about Karababas. Built in the 1600s by Turks to protect the city from the Venetians, the architecture of the place was more Venetian than Turkish, according to her book. She was learning that the entire island was a hodgepodge of cultures, its history jumping from one conquering force to another, one infusion of inhabitants to the next.

At the edge of one of the short, stone walls was a stunning vista of Chalcis. Anita stood next to a group of tourists from the bus and looked beyond the telephone wires and scant trees to the city of white buildings, stacked like Legos, to the soft, brown hills in the distance, to the gradations of blue sky beyond. Layers upon layers, a different view at each turn.

The tour guide, a white-haired gentleman with deep crevices on his tanned face, had called the place Karababa Castle. In her guidebook, it said Fortress of Karababas. Many places in Greece, along with having had many identities throughout history, also had been called many things. There were various spellings and names for almost everything. The city, for example, once called Chalkida, could be spelled as Khalkis, Chalkis, or most commonly now, Chalcis. The island of Euboea might be written

also as Éυυοια or Evia, although it was originally called Negroponte, a name itself which had a confused history as a Greek
phrase interpreted by Italians.

To be honest, she'd had enough of history for the day, and
the tourists standing near her at the fortress's scenic spot
seemed to have turned their attention elsewhere, too. They
talked about lunch, mostly, and where to find a great glass of
ouzo. Anita had eaten her breakfast at the hotel—simple, conti-
nental fare—and she was looking forward to finding a good,
local restaurant for lunch. Back home, she'd ask her son Peter
for recommendations, on the rare occasions she'd find herself in
need of a special place to eat. He checked a website and had
never steered her wrong. But she had no intention of calling
him. In addition to the history of Euboea and Chalcis, she'd also
had quite enough of her adult children for the day.

She hadn't looked at her phone since she left California a
week before. Really, was that so strange? That simple fact had
stupefied Pearl, who was constantly looking at her own phone,
poring over photos and witty things her friends had said. Having
her toast and fruit compote that morning, Anita had finally
pulled her "device" from the recesses of her purse, to find that
she'd never turned it back on after the flight. When she did, it
started to beep and chime endlessly, and she'd almost dropped
it onto her plate trying to find the volume button. Apparently,
also, she'd never pushed "Send" on the text she'd typed Pearl
from the airport. As soon as she did, her phone rang and rang.
She'd had to quickly finish her breakfast, go back to her room,
and suffer through an hour of apologies and explanations to
both Pearl and her brother, Peter, who had been so angry he
could hardly speak.

Really, she did feel bad about it. They'd been so worried. It
wasn't every day—*any day*—she did something like this. But
when she'd heard Peter's tone, the way he had of taking over,

directing her, making demands—and then there was Pearl, whose voice rose to a whiny level reminiscent of her childhood, those times when she had to practice piano, or clean her room, or do anything, really, she didn't feel like doing. Anita loved her children, God knows she did, but speaking to them that morning had taken some of the wind from her sails. And so she changed her plans for the day and bought a ticket for a relaxing tour of the city. It was maybe a little cowardly and not a wholly independent move, but she didn't care.

They filed back onto the bus and the guide began to talk about the Paralia, the central plaza and colonnade visible from her room. They'd find lunch there, he said, in one of the many restaurants along the water's edge. Afterwards, they'd drive the twenty-five kilometers to Eretria, another ancient site.

Anita leaned back in her seat and listened to his deep, assured voice. Just for today, she was happy to be led.

When she arrived in Chalcis that June day so many years ago, the airport was crowded and awash in sunlight. She had a foldable map of Athens she'd found at a bookstore back home and used it to find the train station where, thankfully, someone understood her enough to help buy a ticket to Chalcis. She remembered that the train tracks ran right alongside the water at the Chalcis station. She had Costas's address on a piece of paper and limited cash. This was 1975—no internet, no Google Maps, no cell phones. She'd never had a reason to ask for his phone number. Slinging her backpack over her shoulder, she had started walking.

Outside the tour bus, the countryside streamed by in patches of brown and green. Anita tried to recall details from her earlier journey, but the memories came in short bursts. She remembered walking into a corner store for a sweating bottle of soda and showing the address to the owner. He was wearing an apron, which he untied from his waist and handed to a younger employee. And this man, the first person she met in Greece, walked her all the way to Costas's house.

She was standing on the porch, had just opened her backpack to get something to wipe her face with, when Costas himself walked up.

"Anita," he said, and before she could answer, he had gripped her by the arms and pulled her in for a kiss on either cheek.

His physical presence affected all her senses. Tall and dark, with square shoulders under a striped tee shirt, he wore a citrusy cologne she inhaled as his soft lips pressed in. And the melodious way he said her name felt like a punch in the stomach.

On her best days, on her worst days, Anita would close her eyes and try to remember that first impression, the sheer, life-altering promise of it. This person, this place, this life. The wide streets winding through white storefronts, the neatly porched homes, the absorbing blue of the Grecian sky, like a pure drop of indigo compared to the wishy-washy sky of California (as she then recalled it). She remembered feeling like a life *force*, what people talk about when they talk about youth and the way it pulses through you. Her recollections were time, place, and people, but also: youth, pulsing, her blood alive and coursing and seeking and devouring. Every step progressing towards a new, unknown, exciting destination. The sensation that anything could happen, any day. It was also getting on a plane by herself and flying across the globe. It was Greece and its foreignness; it was past and present and future.

But it was the particular thrill of Costas, to be sure. Wide-smiled, wavy-haired, gentle Costas. He led her by the hand that summer, to places and experiences she couldn't have predicted. He took her in without question and convinced his parents to let her sleep on the couch—his mother, really, as his father was traveling most of the summer for business. Costas had just finished his third year of university and was training to be a teacher. Throughout the summer, he was assisting in a classroom, so he was busy until noon every weekday. His mother also worked, and his sister had married the year before and moved out, so Anita was alone most mornings until he returned. Sometimes, she'd play house and prepare his lunch. Other days, they'd go out. Often, they'd make love and stay in until just before his mother was due home from work.

The bus stopped along the colonnade, and everyone began to file out. The couple from the Netherlands in their matching earth-tone outfits, the family from Spain, the young man and woman who couldn't keep their hands off each other. Anita scooted forward in her seat and waited her turn. There were two other single people on the tour—a woman at least ten years her senior, and a middle-aged man, and at times the three exchanged small smiles of recognition. She liked this aspect of traveling, the people-watching. You never knew exactly what someone's story was, and you were free to imagine.

Soon, she had left the group, with the agreement to meet back on the bus in an hour. She had planned to have a nice, formal lunch but decided instead to grab a sandwich and eat outdoors, by the water. She didn't want to be contained. Near a docked sailboat, she found an empty bench and sat down with her food and another slippery bottle of soda.

Leaving Chalcis the last time was so difficult, yet entirely necessary. Costas would be starting back at school and after three-and-a-half weeks, his mother was losing patience with their long-term guest and perhaps, beginning to worry about having an American daughter-in-law. Anita and Costas shared a tearful goodbye at the curb, where the taxi his mother had called and paid for sat idling. Costas talked about coming to

California in the spring, or possibly the next summer, after he graduated. Anita cried herself nearly sick, all the way to Athens.

There was a sleepy vibe on the tour bus when everyone returned from lunch. Anita thought she could tell who had found ouzo because before the sleepiness descended, there were contained bursts of laughter, a mellow joyfulness. She thought about trips she and her ex-husband took when the kids were young—San Diego, Palm Springs. Usually someplace the kids could splash around while they had tropical drinks. This was before Allen started traveling more and more for his business. For a few years, they had Disneyland passes, but it became hard for her to take the kids on her own. An odd number is never good at an amusement park, when everyone wants to ride with someone else, and when one child (Peter) is adventurous and fearless and the other (Pearl) would wait until the last possible moment to decide she couldn't get on a ride after all.

So many things were ruined by Allen and what he did. As accustomed as Anita had become, after more than twenty years of being divorced, at times it still surprised her to realize their family had broken up. They'd been divorced longer than they were married, and this fact, too, seemed surreal and hard to believe.

When she returned from Greece, she resumed her job at the skating rink. To appease her mother, she enrolled in three classes at the community college, and that's where she met Allen, who was taking general education courses before transferring to pursue a degree in business. At least, that was his plan at the time. He was working at Sears, part-time in the appliance department, when someone approached him about a job with an eyewear distributor. He started working for them, then transferred to an even larger company. He finished an AA degree at the community college, but that was all. The new company offered a great salary, enough to buy the Bellflower house, which was old but good-sized. The children were born. And when Peter was ten and Pearl was eight, Allen took another job, with a French eyewear conglomerate. He started traveling to Paris a few times a year. Anita was thirty-five, and it felt like the American dream was raining down on them, big time. They talked about buying a larger house instead of continuing to renovate the one they had. They talked about Anita returning to school once the kids were a bit older. They talked about taking a trip to Europe for their fifteenth anniversary. Anita mentioned Greece (although she'd never told Allen about Costas); he wanted to see Italy. That trip never happened, either, because by then they were miserable and talking about separation, and of course, unbeknownst to her, he was already making trips to New York to see Jennifer.

What had happened? What could she say now, these many years later? Looking back, she'd been content for a long time. She'd throw herself into motherhood and knew, even as it was happening, that the kids' early years would be the happiest of her life. She thought her marriage went through the same growing pains, the same peaks and valleys, of any other marriage. She supported Allen's endeavors and tried to take care of everything else. They had good sex, they seemed to have reliable communication, the same general goals. She kept herself in good shape, well-groomed.

Oh, what am I doing? she thought. Taking that same road to nowhere. She made a deliberate turn and from some back alley of her mind, brought forward something her mother had said, one of those many weekends when Anita would call after the kids had gone to bed. Maybe she'd been packing more of Allen's things into boxes or had found something else incriminating amongst his new, silk-blend business shirts, maybe she'd woken up, drenched in sweat, straining under the burden of the house, the car, upcoming birthdays, the psychological adjustment of two adolescents, the inevitability of dying alone—whatever it was, she'd called her mom, yet again, for support. And her mother, who had raised three children with the help of what sometimes seemed to be the world's last truly good man, said: "Honey, this is not *your* failing, something lacking in you. You're up late worrying now, but at some point, it will be Allen, lying in his bed and staring at the ceiling, figuring out what was lacking in *him*, wondering what he's done. I can promise you that."

Anita wondered about this, whether Allen had moments of insomnia or regret, and with this wondering came complicated emotions. She appreciated the sentiment of the first part of her mother's reassuring—that nothing was missing in her—but the latter part brought her no ease, because she had loved her husband and probably still did. The thought of his suffering brought her no joy, no relief. And all of it, at times, felt like somebody else's story from long, long ago, a closed chapter, a dream, another life in a fictional time, not unlike that summer in Greece, when she was twenty years old and everything was shiny, vivid, and new, and Anita had lived only for herself.

———

Peter

PETER HEARD noise from within his mother's condo and when he turned the knob, the door was unlocked. He stepped inside. "Hello?"

Pearl appeared at the opening to the living room. "Hey, what are you doing here?"

He took a breath, waited for a moment to respond. It was something the counselor had suggested, this slight pause when he felt impatient or annoyed. "I said I'd reschedule my meeting so you wouldn't have to miss your—what was it?"

She put her hands on her hips. "It was a food drive I was supposed to oversee but remember—I said I had the dates wrong after all? Well, anyway, you're here now. Do you want water? Not much else in the fridge."

Her short skirt made a swishing sound as she walked, and her bright green blouse had come untucked a bit in the back. Peter followed her to the kitchen, nodding a hello to the man kneeled on the living room carpet, fiddling with the television.

"I still don't understand why they couldn't put this off until next week," he said, motioning to the man.

Pearl creased her eyebrows, gave him a signal to be quiet. She had always been over-sensitive about people's feelings. "They're replacing everyone's cable boxes," she said. "Better to do it all at once, I guess. They said something about the liability of coming in here without someone home." She handed him a bottled water and sat down at the dining room table. "You're a lawyer—you should know something about that."

When they were young, they'd always sat at the same seats at this table. Their mother at the end closest to the kitchen, his father at the other, Pearl to his father's left, Peter to his right.

Peter sat down in the closest chair, across from Pearl; they had both assumed their parents' places. "Have you talked to her?" he asked. "Is she still coming back next week?"

Pearl spread her fingers on the table's dark surface. "As far as I know. She said her flight is a week from Wednesday."

Peter shook his head, tried to wait a beat before talking. "Three weeks in Greece. Must be nice."

"I hope it is. About time she did something for herself."

He took a drink of water and when he set the bottle down, a few drops spurted out. "She does all right, I'd say. Buys whatever she wants."

"You're worried about the money she's spending? It's hers."

"No." He looked at Pearl, who was shorter and plumper, and

had her dark hair cut short and tucked behind each ear and still, somehow, managed to look like their flaxen-haired mother. They had the same blue, searching eyes.

"Then what?" she asked.

"It's just irresponsible, running off by herself like that. An older woman, traveling alone."

Pearl's eyes widened, but she didn't speak.

"What would she do in an emergency?" he asked.

"Like what?"

"I don't know." He picked up the water bottle again; it made a crunching sound. "Something medical. What if she runs out of cash?"

"She'd go to a hospital, a bank."

"This doesn't bother you?"

Pearl shrugged. She looked into the kitchen then back at him. "I miss her, but I'm glad she went. Sure, I was upset at first, when we didn't know what had happened."

"You were hysterical," he said.

"Not quite."

The cable repairman stood up and cleared his throat. "All done here, Ma'am." He glanced at Peter. "Sorry for the inconvenience."

"It's no problem at all," Pearl said, smiling. She walked him all the way to the door.

Peter looked at his watch, remembered he was supposed to pick up Reese from football while Tanya saw a movie with her friend.

Pearl reappeared at the table. "Peter," she said, deliberating.

"What?"

"There are things you don't know about Mom, things I didn't know."

His jaw clenched; something cracked painfully. "What's that supposed to mean?" he said. "For God's sake, Pearl, don't get all dramatic on me. I've had a long day already, a long week. If you've got something to tell me, just tell me." Take a breath, he told himself.

She crossed her arms over the bright, green shirt. "I'm only responding to your attitude. What *is* with your attitude, anyway? Can't Mom have something for herself, *do* something for herself?"

"What are these 'things I don't know?'"

"She's more capable than you think," she said. "That's all."

He thought about the times his mother consulted him about household matters, after his father had left. Should they paint the exterior of the house or put it off another year? Could he climb up to the attic and get down the holiday items? Could he drive her to this appointment or that store? Had he talked to his father? Should they have the grass seeded again? He was fifteen!

"You don't have to worry," Pearl said. "She's been to that island before."

"What do you mean, to Greece?"

She grinned. She was enjoying not telling him.

"With Dad?" he asked. "I don't remember—"

"No," Pearl said. "Before they were married." Her eyes sparkled. "She went one summer, when she was young. She met a boy there, well, a young man."

Peter stood up, and the chair squealed along the tiles. He didn't have the patience for the women in his life, he really didn't. "Are you going to get her at the airport, or should I? Let's get it straight this time."

"Aren't you curious at all?"

"About what, Mom's summer romance fifty years ago?"

"Yes."

He looked around the condo, plain and sparse. It was like she never really embraced moving here, hadn't made it cozy or her own. He wondered if his mother was unhappy and if so, why they hadn't noticed. He sat back down. "Was she going to meet that guy, is that it?"

Pearl shrugged. "I don't know. She doesn't know that I know about it. That earlier trip, I mean."

Peter tried to imagine his mother sitting at some Greek café with an elderly man, leaning over glasses of wine or cups of coffee. In a flash, he imagined his wife Tanya in the same situation, face lit by candlelight, dining with another man. He couldn't let that happen. He wouldn't.

"Maybe this move was rougher on her than we thought," Pearl said. "We had so many memories at the house. These substantial changes can be hard for anyone. I don't want to see her upset again. I couldn't take that."

Peter saw the place now, the hospital room with its white walls and beeping machines. She'd had surgery, he remembered, something with her wrist. She'd taken the pain pills for too long. Too many at once. A mistake anyone could make, she said, and their father had agreed. She came home after a couple of days and was the same as she'd ever been, maybe better. It was a mistake, he'd always known that.

He stood up again, this time more carefully so the chair wouldn't make noise. "If you could get her from the airport, that would be great. It's our anniversary next week, and well, work is crazy right now."

"Sure." She followed him to the door as she had the repairman.

They exchanged a hug, and Peter stepped into the bright sunlight. "Thanks," he said.

Pearl nodded, framed in the door of their mother's home, one hand still on the knob. "No problem. Oh, and Peter? Give the boys a hug from their auntie, and enjoy your anniversary, okay?"

But Peter was already half-way to his car, so he raised his

hand, a sort of farewell and acknowledgement in one and as usual, much too small of a gesture for the occasion.

———

Anita

SHE'D BEEN in Euboea for two weeks—one week at the luxurious hotel then another at the more reasonably priced room she'd found down a side street next to a café where she had lunch almost every day. The new room was smaller and lacked the space of the first one, but it had everything she needed, and she liked the way it was snuggled in between the homes and businesses of actual residents. She liked to wake up and hear the sounds of Greeks going about their normal, daily routines.

The café had the best strong coffee she'd ever tasted. She ordered fruit and a pastry some days, a heartier breakfast of seasoned eggs on others. Some days, she slept in and grabbed a banana from a local fruit stand, then saved her appetite for a long, leisurely lunch. Each day, she walked through the city, finding new corners and fresh views. She spent one hot afternoon in the local library, finishing the book she'd brought on the plane. Twice, she swam at a local beach, amongst the families and teenagers, the regulars with their deeply tanned skin. She took a boat tour, along the coastline until they marveled at the area's highest peaks, the Xirón and Teléthrion Mountains, both craggy and majestic against the blue sky. She wore headphones set to English and heard all about the wars, trade, and broken alliances throughout centuries. She may have nodded off.

Sometimes, she thought she could live this way forever. She wasn't accountable to anyone, except for the phone calls from Pearl every few days, and she liked the thought of an empty calendar, the days spread out before her to fill however she chose. She had walked by the house where Costas lived in 1975. She had walked by it many times, in fact, at various times of the day. But she had never mustered the courage to knock. Yesterday, after a lunch of thinly sliced lamb over a bed of lettuce and a tall glass of the local soda she loved, she had walked down that now-familiar street and had watched while a young woman herded three red-haired children down the steps and onto the sidewalk where she and Costas had said their tearful goodbyes. A man, obviously the children's father, came out and waved as they bounced down the street, calling back to him and being pulled in starts and fits by their mother. So this young family now lived in the house where Anita had spent so much time that summer long ago, and there would be no way to catch a glimpse of her pen pal, or to talk to him. Is that what she had planned? She wasn't sure. But now that the possibility of *whatever* she had been thinking was gone, a minor depression set in.

At the library, she had looked through the phone books but for the life of her, could not remember the name of Costas' father. His mother's name was Yvonne, but there was no listing for her, or for Costas. Their surname was a quite popular one, and there were four listings with the initial C and the name, but when she thought about tracking down each of those addresses she began to feel quite foolish. What exactly was the point? Like her, Costas had probably married and had children. He had always wanted to leave the island, so the chances he'd done so were fairly high. Even if he were still in Euboea, he probably wanted to enjoy his senior years without disturbance; certainly, he'd never followed up on visiting her in California and hadn't really kept in touch after that summer.

It was a Tuesday morning in the year 2017, and she was Anita Mullen, formerly Anita Bresler, and she lived in Cerritos, California, in a condo her daughter had found for her. She was a subscriber to the local performing arts center and had a regular, monthly book club. Her two children lived nearby, and her grandsons were sources of endless pride. She liked to read and take long walks. Her parents were both gone. Her ex-husband lived in Idaho. His hair was thinning, and he had rheumatoid arthritis. She had loved being a mother and when the kids got older, she had worked for many years doing secretarial tasks at a local non-profit that supported orphanages in Mexico. Her daughter, Pearl, had also had a series of jobs in the charitable sector. Her son was a successful attorney, and his wife was able to stay home, as Anita had done, to take care of their children. Anita volunteered at her church, in the office, on Mondays. Her close circle of friends, some of them widowed now or still linked to husbands who didn't want to do much, liked to meet for dinners or concerts or plays. Your cultural crew, Pearl called them. She had this life, Anita knew. And yet, here she was, pretending to be a local of this sunny island in Greece, sipping coffee as the morning broke into day, watching people walk by as she stayed and stayed and stayed.

After seeing the young family at Costas's former house, Anita had booked her return flight. One week from tomorrow, she thought. It seemed, at once, like a richness of days and at the same time, not nearly enough. After she bought the ticket, she had even had a phone call from Peter, explaining that he was taking Tanya on a surprise trip to Catalina Island for their anniversary and wouldn't be able to pick her up. He'd see her a few days after her return, he said. Anita had been touched by his call and gladdened that he'd finally agreed to take some time off work. In many ways, he was his sister's opposite. Pearl, who tended to act on her feelings much more than was practical. But who was Anita to judge, remaining indulgently in Greece, on a whim, on a prayer?

She finished the last of the good, strong coffee and picked up her shawl. It was blue and green and beaded with iridescent bits, and Anita had bought it from a woman with a cart near Negroponte Bridge. This was Euboea's most famous spot, the unique draw bridge she remembered from her earlier trip. Here, the "mad waters" of the city churned and swirled, and the current changed direction every six hours. Tourists lined up along the banks to see this phenomenon, caused by the pull of the moon. Anita wrapped the shimmering material around her shoulders and stood up.

On the narrow sidewalk outside the café, a young man hurried past. Anita watched him. Tall, a head of dark hair—not remarkable here—but something about the set of his shoulders, the rhythm of his gait, struck a chord. When he turned to look into the café window, her heart stopped. She fumbled in her wallet for money and threw down the first bill she touched. Hurrying outside, she caught a glimpse of the young man as he rounded a corner. She followed for two blocks, as he adjusted his hair in the reflective glass of a butchery, as he waved to someone in a tailor shop, as he bounded up the steps to the door of a small, attached home just one street over from where Costas had lived. Because, of course Anita had chosen a hotel in proximity to this place, had sat at the café over and over hoping to see something, *someone* from that summer. This young man, perhaps still a teenager, obviously couldn't be her old pen pal, but he reminded her so startlingly of him, his posture, his expression; he brought Costas to mind in the same way her grandson brought Allen forward—in stark relief, without warning.

The young, dark-haired man knocked on the door of the home and in a few moments, it opened. Anita stood across the street, leaning against the cool stone of a building, shielding her eyes from the afternoon sun. Too late, she'd realized she left her sunglasses at the café.

A figure appeared on the step, shadowed by the light coming in from the windows behind him. It was a man—that was apparent—and as he stepped outside, Anita recognized the slow, hesitant moves of someone older. The two embraced, and the tenderness of the older man's hand on the younger's shoulder, the deference in the young man's bowed head—this wordless but apparent bond struck a familiar chord in Anita. The younger man stepped aside and the older—probably his grandfather, she realized—raised his eyes and looked directly at Anita. After a few moments, he lowered his head and went back inside.

Anita lingered in the street, enjoying the coolness of the wall against her back, listening to the sounds of cars, a multitude of voices, and sandaled feet slapping the hot concrete. And when she started walking again, in the direction of the café to retrieve her sunglasses, a small, contented smile lingered at the corners of her mouth.

———

Giorgos

HE'D BE late for his eye exam, that much was certain. He loved the boy, everyone knew that, but the boy could be lazy and forgetful, and Giorgos had lost count how many times he'd told his daughter this.

I know, Papa, I know. He's young, give him time.

When *he* was that age, he'd already completed his apprenticeship, after working up the nerve to stand up to his father.

He checked the clock again. If the boy came now, they'd have twenty minutes to walk over. They'd have to hurry a little, but the boy's legs were strong, and he was tall as his father had been, as Giorgos himself had been, in another life. Now, he was shrinking, and he had to remind himself to stand erect. He could take himself to the damn eye appointment if it weren't for the surgery. Now, he could barely see from one eye, and it threw everything off.

There it was—a forceful, unhesitant knock. His heart warmed, despite his aggravation with the boy. When he opened the door, so opened his heart, even more. Because the boy was magnificent, all white teeth and broad shoulders, and wasn't he a good boy for attending to his grandfather when he could be out chasing girls? Giorgos clapped the boy on his firm back, reached up to enfold him.

Over the boy's shoulder, he noticed a woman standing across the street. Draped in a blue cloth, her eyes like two gems that he could tell, even at the distance and with his bad eye, were also blue. Her hair was blonde and short. He looked at her and for a moment, he was back in Amsterdam, those months he went to study his craft, those nights with Elise, a blonde waitress with plans to enter the royal army when she turned nineteen. The colors of the city swam before him—the red and blue bicycles, the garnet brick above green water, the undulating flag with its equal stripes of red, white, and blue. The amber glasses of beer, the gray night skies, so full of dampness and promise, and so different from the vivid blue back home in Greece.

Giorgos turned back towards his house, chuckling a little to himself. Old man, he chided, those were good days but now, here you are. Get a hold of yourself. Carefully, he walked along the scuffed, wooden floor. In the kitchen, his grandson was looking for something to eat, and Giorgos smiled again, listening to the vigorous sounds of the younger man's foraging.

BAD LUCK

THEY BARELY SPOKE on the drive over. Somewhere past Corona, as urban sprawl gave way to great, rolling hills of green, Ashley reclined her seat, bunched her hoodie into a pillow, and fell asleep.

Sam tried to focus on the road. Here, he had arranged this weekend at the beach, had called in a favor to get two nights completely free at the hotel where his cousin worked, and she couldn't even keep him company during the drive? Sure, they'd both been putting in long hours, between classes at UC Riverside and jobs. Ashley was still waitressing at The Cheesecake Factory, and he'd had a research internship since January. They were both wiped. This weekend would be one last chance to relax before the crush of exams, the finale of graduation, moving, starting jobs.

Cruising through the mountains—expansive green spotted with wildflowers in purple, orange and yellow—Sam was surprised, as always, by the vast amount of unspoiled land. Looking at all that space made it hard to imagine the planet being overpopulated.

Traffic was light through Orange County, and when they

were ten miles from San Clemente, Sam shook Ashley's shoulder. He swept aside the blonde hair that had fallen over her face.

She stretched, making little noises, and sat up. "Sorry," she said, blinking.

"No," he said. "I'm glad you got some rest." A flash: that night, her laughs echoing down the empty street. He pushed the memory away.

To their right, the Pacific Ocean stretched and sparkled. They drove for a while in silence and looked.

"Do you think the water will be cold?" Ashley asked.

He nodded. "It's only April. But we can go for walks, and the hotel has a heated pool and hot tub."

"I can't wait," she said.

"There's free breakfast in the morning. Probably, we could grab enough for a light lunch." He didn't want her to think he was being cheap, and yet, neither of them was rolling in cash. The student life.

Shortly, the GPS announced their exit.

"Where does your cousin go again?" she asked.

"Community college. He graduated from high school last year."

"It's so nice of him to get us a room."

"We have to call him when we get there. He'll meet us in the parking garage." He glanced at her. "Obviously, we have to lay low all weekend."

She grinned, her lips shiny and pink with gloss. "What, no loud, all-night parties at the pool?"

There were a thousand caustic things he could say to that, but he just smiled. *No*, he wanted to say, *it seems you do most of your hard partying without me.* It was hard to believe he'd been thinking of surprising her with a ring at graduation. Now, everything was confused.

In the hotel parking lot, Sam's cousin gave them the room

keys. They each grabbed a duffel and went inside. On the third floor, their room was the final one. They walked down the long hallway, faded carpet with a pattern of scrolls and dots, and Sam watched Ashley. There were so many things about her he loved. Her low-pitched laugh, the feel of her fingers in his hair. She had a way of throwing back her shoulders before a challenging task, a tilt to her walk when she'd been drinking. He shook his head, remembering.

They went into the room, and Ashley's eyes widened. Quietly, she jumped up and down. It was a suite, with a living room section in the front—couch, TV, fridge—and a bedroom in the back. From the small balcony, they could see a narrow strip of ocean over the freeway.

She fell back onto the bed, and the bulky bedspread seemed to rise and cushion her on both sides. She looked small and precious, a colorful pulse in the still life of the room.

"This is so great," she said. "What do you want to do?"

Sam cocked an eyebrow and climbed over her as she laughed.

———

IN THE MORNING, they woke up at eight o'clock and lounged until nine. They pulled on sweatpants, and Sam put a baseball cap over his thick, messy hair before they went downstairs for the free breakfast.

It was the typical spread: cereals, hot and cold, bread and fruit, a waffle maker. Ashley went straight for the vat of oatmeal, and Sam found what remained of the scrambled eggs under a big, circular warmer. He was debating having that, or making himself a waffle, when a man behind them starting chatting up Ashley.

"We came over from Riverside," she was saying. "We're both at the UC."

"That's great," a deep voice said. "Just great. What are you studying?"

"I'm a Public Policy major, and my boyfriend is Biochemistry."

"Is this him?"

Sam had made his way over with a plate of eggs, after dodging a family of four fighting at the breakfast cereal cylinders.

"Yes."

"Hey there, fella." The man was old, probably in his fifties, with thin but combed gray hair. He wore khakis, a trendy tee shirt, and black flip flops. He had a paunch and a ruddy complexion.

"Hey," Sam said. "How you doing?"

"I've been better, I can tell you that." He reached over to grab his toast, which had just popped up. "Your girl tells me you're having a weekend getaway." There was an accent in his voice, eastern-US, but Sam couldn't place it.

"Something like that."

"Are you from around here, John?" Ashley stood at the fruit section, waiting for a woman to finish selecting chunks of cantaloupe.

"Actually, I live nearby." He was using a black walking stick, the kind with a rubber tip, and he pointed it towards the window, beyond the pool outside. "I have a big house in the hills there. Very grand."

Inwardly, Sam rolled his eyes. Of course this man staying at the Best Western had a grand house.

"But I've been having some bad luck," the man said.

Ashley turned from the fruit, a pair of metal tongs held aloft. "What happened?"

He set his plate down. There was only a hard-boiled egg and the toast on it. He looked at her intently, leaned in. "A couple of weeks ago, I woke up in the middle of the night when the fire alarm went off. The house is quite large, three levels on that hill. There are hundreds of steps. Stairs, you see?"

She nodded.

"I got out of bed and headed to the kitchen to shut off the alarm." He took a breath. "The house is exceptionally large, very grand, and the central staircase is Italian marble. I forget what kind, but it was a big selling point, I can tell you. It's breathtaking."

Sam sidestepped Ashley to get a cup of coffee from one of the large thermoses at the end of the counter. The man waited for him to turn back around before he continued, so Sam felt trapped there, listening to him.

"The alarm's going off—seems even louder with all that tile —and my wife is sound asleep through it, somehow. I reach the top of those stairs, and the noise is deafening, really unbelievable, even in that massive house. And on the first step, my foot slips like there's butter, and I fall about fifteen steps."

Ashley covered her mouth with her hand and looked down at the walking stick.

"If you can believe it, I was fine." He raised his shoulders and eyebrows at the same time.

It's a New York accent, Sam thought, but there's something diluted about it.

"Some bruising, a sore hip. A pretty good headache for a couple of days. Doctor says because I was half asleep, I didn't fight during the fall. That helped me from getting injured in lots of ways."

"Wow," Ashley said. "And that's why you have a cane? I'm sorry, is it a cane?"

He grabbed a banana, pulling it forcefully from the bunch,

and put it on his plate. "Sure, it's a cane. You can see that. But it wasn't from the fall." He paused, shook his head as though he couldn't believe what he was about to say. "More bad luck. Last week, in my backyard, I got bit by a rattlesnake." Gingerly, he pulled up his pant leg and they saw two swollen, angry red areas, outlined in a black marker.

"Ouch," Ashley said, making a face.

"You should've seen it a few days ago," he said. "My calf was twice this size."

"Are there normally snakes in your yard?" Sam asked.

"I never saw any," he said. "But they're native, that's for sure."

"But why are you here?" Ashley asked.

He laughed, and the hard-boiled egg jiggled precariously on his plate. "My wife told me, Baby, I'll visit my mother. We have two kids—five and seven—and they're climbing all over me, never let me rest." He looked at Sam. "My wife's younger and when they are, they want kids." He shrugged. "Anyhow, she took them to her mother's and doesn't know I'm here. I'm having a pest control place work in the back yard. It's a large lot, a massive house, you see, and it'll take them a few days. I didn't want to argue with the wife about it—they said the stuff they use is fine around kids—but you know women, always worrying. And I figure I come down here and avoid all those steps. Hard for me to manage with this thing." He tapped the tip of the walking stick on the ground.

"Well, take care," Sam said. "Ash, I'll get a table."

"I'll be right there." She turned back to the man. "I hope your luck gets better."

"You and me both, sugar. You and me both."

———

THEY GRABBED BAGELS, fruit, and yogurt and packed everything in Ashley's purse for their lunch. The beach was about a mile away, through a residential section and some good-sized hills. They took two blankets from the hotel and used one over, one under, because the day was sunny but cool. Ashley couldn't stop talking about the man. She had googled rattlesnake bites and kept trying to show Sam disgusting photos. All in all, not the romantic time he had imagined. In the afternoon, they went back to the hotel and took a nap. Ashley wanted pizza for dinner, so they went to a place a couple of miles down the road and were back early for a soak in the hot tub before it closed. In the hotel room, they had changed into their swimsuits before Ashley realized she'd left her phone in the car.

Sam pressed against her, placing his hands on either side of her hips. Her skin was cool to the touch, the string of her bikini bottom pressing gently into the softness. "What will you give me if I run down and get your phone?" He pulled her closer.

She was busy pulling her hair into some sort of plastic clip, and her left elbow almost collided with his chin. She squirmed under his hands. "How about my eternal gratitude?"

"Not exactly what I had in mind."

"A hand-written thank you note?"

"Hm," he said, releasing her. "I'll be right back."

As he waited for the elevator, he tapped his heel on the gaudy carpet. He felt unsettled, anxious. Already, he was thinking about his classes on Monday and his work at the lab. He'd been interning for a pharmaceutical biochemistry group that tested drugs, food, and other products. He analyzed samples and kept up the laboratory, which included monitoring inventory but also several tasks that could only be called janitorial. The best part, for sure, was working with samples. There was something so practical, so clear, about measuring chemicals and applying them, something so uncomplicated about looking through a microscope and breaking down what you saw within clear, stated parameters. Other interns complained about the repetitiveness of the work, but Sam found a focus, a sustained calm, when he was bowed over the lens.

The hotel elevator opened, and he walked through the lobby into the covered parking garage. It occurred to him that he could look through Ashley's phone to see who she'd been texting lately. He wondered if she still had the same passcode, or whether she'd changed it. Once, at the beach, she'd been scrolling through something and laughed. When he asked about it, she said it was nothing. Another time, he thought he heard the chime of a text when she went into the bathroom. This is crazy, he told himself, at the same moment he knew he'd try to look at her messages anyway.

As he approached his car, he noticed another car idling near the mouth of the garage, a figure bent over at the driver-side window.

"You know you don't mean that," a deep voice said.

"Leave me alone." A woman's voice came from inside the car. "I'm wasting my time here."

"Come on, sugar. Park the car and have a drink with me."

Sam realized it was John, the rattlesnake victim from breakfast. He glanced over to confirm and now saw the cane, propped at an angle near the car's front wheel. As he watched, the women inched the car forward, and John almost lost his balance straightening up and backing away.

"You're going to run me over!" he yelled.

"I might," she yelled back.

He swung the cane, and the rubber tip smacked bluntly against the car door.

The tires squealed as the woman accelerated. At the turn of the driveway, Sam caught a glimpse of her: dark hair, big sunglasses.

"Asshole!" she shouted before the car disappeared.

Sam reached in and found Ashley's phone in the groove between the two front seats. He pressed the button and looked at the screensaver: Ashley and a female friend puckering in front of a waterfall. The picture was from the summer before. Why didn't she have a photograph of her boyfriend, of *him*, to look at every time she picked up her phone?

"Hey there."

He looked up and John was waiting for him at the hotel door. Slowly, he walked over, squinting in the bright sunlight coming from the windowed lobby.

"Sorry about that," John said. He wore the same khakis as the day before, with a white shirt that was more unbuttoned than buttoned, exposing his tanned but flabby chest.

"No worries," Sam said, stepping around him.

"If I had a dollar for every time a woman almost ran me over, I'd have a villa in Italy, I can tell you that." He laughed and limped into the lobby.

They stood at the elevator. Sam pushed the button. It seemed the guy was waiting for him to say something. "Was she mad you're here?" he asked.

"What?"

"Your wife," Sam said. "You said she didn't know you were at the hotel—"

The door to the elevator opened, and a young couple stepped off, wearing beach attire and holding hands.

"Brother," John said, lowering his voice. "That wasn't my wife." As Sam stepped into the elevator, he gave him a playful punch on the shoulder.

Sam inhaled, looked at the man's smug, reddened face. "Oh."

"You go ahead," the man said. "I'm going to drive up to my house and get a few things." He winked as the door closed. "Don't do anything I wouldn't do."

Muted, jazzy music filled the elevator. As Sam stared at the colorful advertising posters on the wall, photos of people in all states of relaxation and enjoyment, his chest tightened. A flash: Ashley and that guy, walking down the street towards her apartment as Sam stood in the streetlight. He'd been calling and calling, worried after she left a party and didn't return his texts. He'd driven over to check on her, to make sure she was safe. He'd backed behind the side of the building when he saw her, had watched as she stumbled and giggled, holding onto the guy's arm. He'd left after they kissed against a car, after they groped each other before going inside. Later, Ashley swore nothing had happened. Too much to drink, she claimed, and the guy left after he dropped her at the apartment door. But he'd seen for himself and this, she didn't know.

———

THE NEXT MORNING, they saw John again at the breakfast buffet. He was seated at a table and waved them over. Sam opened his mouth to say something to Ashley, but she had already signaled that they'd join him.

"You won't believe it," John said before niceties, before they'd even sat down. "I had a phone call from the pest control."

Ashley set her oatmeal and juice down. "Did they find the snake?"

"Snake?" He slapped his hands on the table and the silverware jangled. "They found a dozen so far!"

Sam took a breath and pulled out his chair. How their fates had become aligned with this guy, he had no idea.

"Wow," Ashley said, pouring milk into her bowl of oatmeal. "They had a nest maybe?"

John sipped his coffee. "That's the weird thing, and I don't know what to think about this."

She nodded, encouraging him to continue.

"They said there were a couple different types, and one of them isn't native to this area at all."

"Maybe someone had one for a pet and lost it?" Sam said.

"They suggested that," John said. "But to have them show up so suddenly is strange. The guy from pest control said rattlesnakes make a den, usually in a rocky area, like a cliff or something, and they can use the same den from generation to generation, for like a hundred years."

"So did they find a den in your yard?" Ashley asked.

"Hell, no! That house is only eight years old." He winked at Sam. "I used to live back east, you see, but I've been here so long I can't remember snow anymore. I had a business that failed, a marriage that failed. Move west, young man!" He laughed. "And I've had nothing but success on this coast. Thriving business, beautiful women. Trophy house for a trophy wife. We put in all the landscaping when we bought it."

"I don't understand," Sam said. "Where did the snakes come from?"

John leaned back and crossed his arms. "He said it was almost like somebody dumped them, right in my yard. Talk about your bad luck. I hadn't been back there for months myself. My wife asked me to check out a section of rotting fence. She said the kids had found it, and she was worried they'd climb through or get splinters or something. I wasn't going to fix it myself, you see, but I had to know what to tell the workmen."

They sat quietly for a few moments, eating. Sam picked at his eggs, separating the undercooked parts from the rest. He thought about the night before, after they'd sat in the hot tub. When he'd finished his shower, Ashley was asleep already, rolled up into a child-like ball on her side of the bed. He'd watched television for a while, unable to shake the feeling she was only pretending to sleep.

Slowly, John stood up, pressing his cane firmly into the carpet. "I'll leave you lovebirds to your breakfast. Life's full of surprises, isn't it?" He smiled, his lips stretching to white.

"Have a good day," Ashley told him.

After he'd gone, Sam lowered his voice. "He's so full of it, isn't he?"

"What do you mean?"

"I saw him yesterday in the parking garage. He was fighting with some woman he said wasn't his wife."

"So?"

Sam set down his fork. "So, maybe it was his wife who put the snakes in the yard and told him to go out there."

She sputtered orange juice. "What? You're crazy."

He leaned back in his chair, stewing. On the other side of the wide doors, which had been opened to let in the morning breeze, two kids ran around the pool, shooting each other with water pistols. Sam listened to the sound of their high voices and the pats of their sneakers on the cement. "I got you," one said. "You missed," the other claimed.

Ashley put her hand on his forearm. "Sam."

He shook himself from his thoughts, which had little to do with the children outside and much to do with that night, the image of Ashley's hair being held in a clump by someone else's fist, her face raised and grinning.

"It was really so nice of you to plan this weekend," she said.

He looked at her and realized she was nervous. Her shoulders were straight as a board.

"So many things are about to change in our lives," she said. "You'll be finishing your internship all summer. After graduation, I need to get serious about finding a place in LA."

"I thought you were thinking about commuting for a while," he said, lamely.

"I'm not sure," she said. "I want to live on my own for a while."

"Okay," he said. "I don't know where I'll be after the summer either. I'm sure they'll make an offer at the lab but if they don't—"

"I mean, I also think we should take a break for a while." She lifted her hand from his arm. "Until we figure out where we'll land."

He stared at her, processing. When he spoke, he couldn't control his voice. "*You're* breaking up with *me*?"

"What's that supposed to mean?"

"Unbelievable," he said.

"Oh, God." She pushed her bowl into the middle of the table and threw the paper napkin on top. "Again with that night? This isn't about that."

"About what?"

"Nothing," she said.

"You're lying," he said.

The children came in from the pool area and joined their parents at a table in the corner. A whiff of sunscreen followed them as they passed by.

"I think it's for the best," Ashley said. "Neither one of us knows where we're going, where this is going."

"I thought I did," Sam said.

"What does that mean?"

"Forget it."

The children walked by again, this time pulling both parents by their hands. They pointed and pulled, the parents following and soon enough, looking where they were signaling. And then Sam saw it and a moment later, smelled it. High on the hilltop, a funnel of black smoke rose into the hazy sky. Slowly, the remaining few diners caught on. An elderly woman walked outside to see; the young beach-clad couple Sam had seen the day before moved to a table closer to the windows and started taking pictures. The smoke cut through the day like an ink stain, spreading and wavering, spoiling the picturesque view of a blooming hillside dotted with opulent houses, all pastels and glass facing the ocean.

Sam looked at Ashley, who was watching the smoke with what almost looked like excitement. He realized, at that moment, that the only aspect of the breakup bothering her was having to tell him.

John appeared at the door to the breakfast room. His ruddy face was a marriage of incredulity and horror. He held his phone in one hand, his cane in the other. The phone was beeping constantly, but he didn't seem to notice. Sam watched as slowly, he made his way to the windows. The cane squeaked as he passed, its rubber tip leaving quickly fading impressions on the busy carpet. A few feet from the opened patio doors, John stopped and looked, mouth agape, and Sam knew then that the thing burning was his house, his very grand house with the staircase of Italian marble. Sam imagined that staircase, still standing tomorrow amidst the ashen ruins. He wondered if John realized that he was supposed to be in the house, partially hobbled.

"Let's go," he said to Ashley. And when she stood up, he guided her, gently, from the room, one hand in its familiar spot on her lower back while his eyes searched for available exits.

WHAT YOU KNOW

JASPER WASN'T the sort of man who liked to share his food, never had been. This did not sit well with women. They always wanted "just a bite" of this and "a taste" of that and sometimes, he knew, they wanted to share an entrée to stay on their diets even though afterwards, they'd order a rich dessert, and he would go home hungry. But these are lessons you learn, especially over the course of a sixteen-year marriage. Maybe it wasn't *all* women who did this but only his wife. He'd forgotten most of the particulars of anyone who'd come before.

He watched as Pamela excavated a gooey slab of brie from what was becoming a deflated, whitish husk. A tendril of cheese hung from the sesame cracker as it made its way to her open mouth. The bistro had opened in a nearby strip mall earlier in the year. There was a section with foreign cheeses and a curated selection of wine, and a small stage where two- or three-piece bands played on weekend nights. Usually folk music or acoustic, slowed-down rock, always with a husky-voiced, middle-aged singer who seemed resigned to be there. Tables were scattered around the rest of the place—some high and round with tall stools, some low and rectangular with benches—adding to the feeling that the place was unsure of what it wanted to be.

This night was a Wednesday. Jasper plucked a black grape from the corner of the wooden board on which their food had been served. Pamela was drinking a Meritage, and her brown eyes had become soft and glossy. She was making short work of the cheese plate, leaving only the prosciutto and smoked Gouda for him, both of which she said left a bad taste. He reached out and grasped her hand. God help him, he loved this woman.

"Tim's trainer was out again this week," she said, arching one eyebrow. "That young guy subbed again."

Tim was their fourteen-year-old son, who played tennis on his high school team and took expensive, private lessons twice a week. The lessons, Jasper thought. The mortgage, the car payments, the insurance. Jenny in braces still. Jenny was their daughter, twelve years old.

"He likes him, though," Jasper said.

Pamela shrugged. She put a walnut into her mouth and looked over at the stage.

He followed her gaze. Two men were untangling the black cords scattered around. One held a guitar on his lap, and the other sat before a keyboard. It seemed there would be a rare, mid-week performance.

"I dragged Jenny into the Goodwill today," Pamela said. "She needs a skirt for Colonial Day at school. She wanted me to get a pattern and sew one for her, because that's what Emma's mom is doing."

"Emma's mom doesn't have a job," he said.

"Exactly." She leaned back, holding her wine glass against her chest.

They'd chosen one of the high tables; they were both tall and long-legged. Jasper glanced at the shadowed triangle under his wife's business skirt as she leaned back and crossed her legs. Pamela had just started classes at the local university to get her MBA. She'd quit her job in sales when the kids were born but had gone back to work once they were in school all day. Her recent promotion to regional supervisor had ignited further aspirations, all of which required an advanced degree. They'd had long talks about how they'd manage with her away three evenings a week. The kids were old enough to get home from school and stay alone until Jasper finished work. If he ran late, they had a neighbor who could check in on them and keep an eye on the house. A few times (such as this Wednesday), Jasper was still at work when Pamela's class ended at eight o'clock, and they'd meet at the bistro for a quick glass of wine if things seemed under control at home. Ironically, these occasional, brief date nights were an unexpected perk during a time they'd imagined they would see less of each other.

The MBA, Jasper thought. And again: the mortgage. The college funds that hadn't grown as much as they'd hoped, Tim's upcoming tennis trip to New York, the cars, the taxes. I'll tell her, he thought. And then, just as quickly: No, nothing will come of it.

Steve and Jasper had been friends since college, and their accounting firm had grown from a partnership handling mostly individual returns to the corporation they had today: six accountants and two secretaries in an office space they rented on the fourth floor of a new building. For years, they'd been in a smaller office but had upgraded to the larger space sixteen months before. Livia was a new secretary, having replaced an older woman who'd retired after years with the company. A dark-haired beauty with tawny skin and the brightest white teeth Jasper had ever seen, Livia kept a group of miniature plastic horses on her desk, and she was industrious and punctual. At least, she had been until recently, when she'd turned in her termination and filed a sexual harassment complaint against him.

On the small stage, a woman in a long, patterned skirt perched on a wooden stool. She put her hands, studded with rings, around the microphone. The first guitar strums caused an instant hush; heads turned.

Pamela set down her empty glass and leaned across the table. "Bridge over Troubled Water," she said.

Jasper glanced again at the woman in her multiple, beaded necklaces and long skirt that was actually rather colonial-looking. "Fleetwood Mac," he said.

His wife leaned back, shaking her head. "You have to say which song," she said.

As it turned out, they were both wrong. It was "Do Right Woman," a rather nice version, Jasper noticed, but by then they were already on their way out.

He thought about telling Pamela in the parking lot, before she remembered she'd left her sweater back in the classroom. He thought about the important thing, that he had never cheated on her, had never really considered the possibility, which should be good for something. He thought about Livia, who was, to some extent, unstable and delusional. He thought about the flirting, which had seemed harmless. The close passes in the hallway, her excuses to find him alone in his office, the eventual, overt gesture he'd rebuffed. He'd encouraged her; he could see that now. He'd enjoyed the attention, young and eager as she was, and if she took his arm that time at a conference or accepted a ride home when she'd had too much Chardonnay at happy hour, well, those were his mistakes. He thought she needed someone to talk to.

The firm's attorney insisted it wouldn't be a problem. Livia had a history of leaving jobs, other court cases filed along the way. And yet Jasper couldn't think of any feasible way to keep it

188 | RESONANT BLUE AND OTHER STORIES

from his wife. Everything was at risk: his company, his marriage, his conflict-free life.

"Ride with me," Pamela said. The university was two miles away. "It's still early. I can show you my classroom, then we'll come back and get your car."

He sat next to her in the new Corolla, purchased to celebrate her promotion. The car payments, he thought. The mortgage. His life with Pamela. She filled the space next to him, smelling of flowers and linen. When she smiled, her teeth appeared faintly red under the amber parking lot lights. Jasper looked at her capable hands, evenly spaced on the leather steering wheel. She was strong, always had been.

They left the strip mall parking lot, turned into a steady stream of traffic. Pamela pulled the car to the yellow line of an intersection, hesitated, then moved forward to make a left turn.

I'll tell her, he thought. He put his hand on her thigh, letting the tips of his fingers drift underneath the creased hem of her skirt. And at that crucial moment, he leaned his head against the headrest and closed his eyes. It had been a long day.

Pamela was in the process of rotating the steering wheel with her left hand, bringing her right up and over while keeping her eyes on the concrete island she'd maneuver around, when the late-model Mercedes came through the intersection at seventy miles per hour. She never saw it, and neither did her husband, who, behind closed eyelids, was thinking about their daughter's orthodontic bill and wondering how much they still owed.

———

DANIEL STACKED the pages on the lectern and looked out over the classroom. The silence extended, weighty and sharp.

Mr. Brooks cleared his throat. "What was the title?"

He looked at the front page, where it was typed. "Wednesday Wine," he said.

The professor rose from the back of the classroom and came forward. "Why don't you take a seat while we wait for comments?"

Daniel walked around the desks, which extended in a wide half-circle, until he found his. The seat creaked in protest when he sat down.

"So what did we think?" Mr. Brooks tilted his body to retrieve the plastic cup of water he kept on the lower shelf of the lectern. The cup had a plastic straw, and Daniel thought he looked like a pale, bearded baby as he took a long sip.

Alyssa sat four desks down on his left. She wore cheetah-print glasses and had three kids at home she was always glad to escape, as she'd told them many times. She reminded Daniel of his aunt, Lisa, who was also in her mid-to-late thirties and harried with children. "The details here are spot on," Alyssa said. "I mean, really, I felt like I was sitting in that wine bar, or bistro, or whatever it was."

A few heads nodded in agreement.

"And there was a true energy between the couple, a zing."

Mr. Brooks looked up. "A what?"

"You know," she said, wiggling her fingers in the air. "Zing."

Thin laughter came in spurts throughout the room.

"In fact," she continued, emboldened. "I wanted to see what happened with them." She leaned forward, pushed her funky glasses up. "That whole sexual harassment thing was introduced, so I was expecting something to develop there—" Her voice trailed off.

Brandon, a tall, chubby guy who wrote explicit sex scenes into every story, spoke. "I agree with you. Why introduce something only to leave it hanging like that?" He shrugged. "Or is this a first chapter?"

Daniel looked at Mr. Brooks. Technically, when someone's story was being workshopped, they weren't supposed to speak.

"You can answer that," the professor said.

"It's a story," Daniel said. His face was burning. It was too warm for the sweater he'd worn, the classroom being small and crowded and aflame with fluorescent light. "Nothing happened with the other stuff because, well, because of the accident. I thought that was obvious."

More nods, less enthusiastic.

"I think what they're getting at, Daniel," Mr. Brooks said, "is that maybe you could—and we're not writing by committee here, not at all—but maybe you could consider moving the story beyond the Wednesday night and maybe not have the accident."

"Because they're great characters," Alyssa said. She gave him a self-satisfied, pitying smile.

Lorna, a thin, mousy woman who didn't speak up much, leaned forward. "I liked the evoking of the colonial skirts, both the daughter and the folk singer." She held an old-fashioned pencil—wooden, green—in her hand and tapped the eraser silently on her desk. "It's as if everyone's moving to a new, scary place. Like pioneers."

Dean, an aspiring science fiction writer with no patience for symbolism or metaphor, shook his head. "They didn't go anywhere," he said, "except the grave. Again."

"Daniel, just keep at it," Mr. Brooks said. "That's the important thing. Don't worry about where it's going."

As the class filed out, the professor called him over. Daniel went and stood next to the white board, which held the graffiti of the night's lesson: context, imagery, falling action. He'd taken careful notes and would type them up later. He was in his third year of college, but had only recently declared a Creative Writing major, having switched from Accounting and before that, Art History. Aunt Mathilde did not enthusiastically approve of the new course of study, but she had no choice because the college fund was under his direct control.

After the final student had exited, Mr. Brooks stroked his beard and leaned on the lectern. "I want you to know, there is no question of whether you can write. Everyone here can write, and you are among the most talented."

Daniel cleared his throat; the skin prickled along his neck. "Thank you."

"All writers get fixated from time to time. Things happen. We have to work them out. Isn't that right?"

He shrugged.

"Hell, look at Proust. Thousands of pages about his child-hood—the house guests, every detail of the sights and smells around him, both in the house and outside in nature. That damn madeleine. But when a theme interferes with the arc of a story, we must ask ourselves if we're making sense of it. Autobi-ography can stifle if you let it. Much more liberating, sometimes, to write *outside* of our experience. Does that make some sort of sense to you, Daniel?"

He was suffocating in the goddamn sweater; the waistline of his jeans was damp with sweat. "I don't believe I'm fixated," he said.

Mr. Brooks nodded, rubbing his lips together. "Very well. Let's try something for argument's sake. You've submitted three stories this semester. Choose one and write a different ending— merely for the exercise of it. See if you can find your way to a different conclusion."

Daniel looked over Mr. Brooks's head to where one of the fluorescent lights was flickering and buzzing softly. "Maybe I could rewrite 'Heavenly Mountain,'" he said, quietly.

"The one with the ski accident?"

"Yes, about the couple who had grown apart, and didn't know how to get back—"

"You see, that *was* interesting, the dynamic between them. Continue with those characters. See what happens next."

"Without the accident?"

"Yes. Can you try that?"

Daniel agreed and promised to have the new draft before the next class. As he left the building and walked home, however, the pungent night air pressed in from all sides, lush green and blooms and bark, overwhelming all else, and his mind wandered to abstract feelings and places, and when he surfaced, back on the sidewalk, he realized he had no idea how to proceed.

———

"HOW WAS CLASS?" Jane stretched out on the bed, her long legs in a V, her feet hanging over the edges. She looked at him over her shoulder.

"Mr. Brooks talked to me afterwards."

"That's good?"

"Not really."

She closed her book and sat up.

"He wants me to rewrite the ending of one of the stories," Daniel said.

"You can do that."

"I'm not sure how to end it." He ran his fingers through his hair. "They don't tell you what to write, only to make it different. This is how I wanted it in the first place."

"But he's a writer, with all those books published. The whole purpose of the class is to learn from him."

"I know."

She patted the mattress next to her, and he sat down. She started rubbing his shoulders.

He could do it; he had to do it. He leaned into her. Jane.

Blonde, tall, unbelievably smart. She'd be a surgeon someday, the head of a prestigious hospital. Or she'd lead a team of researchers, discover a cure for something. What in the world was she doing with him?

"Do you want to go out tomorrow night?" she asked.

He stood up. Her last night, before twelve weeks in Boston for an internship.

"We could see a movie or have a nice dinner. I liked that wine bistro. Do you want to go there again?"

"It'll be crowded on the weekend," he said.

Jane patted his back and reclined on her side, propping her head up. "Your aunt called earlier," she said. "Said to tell you your room is always available. She's so nice. She's been working on her tennis game to compete with you, and the association redecorated the clubhouse. Ping pong and foosball. You love foosball!"

"Great."

"You have this summer course, all those parties off campus. Weekends with home cooking and recreational activities, if you want." She smiled broadly, gamely.

He made a noise, something between a snicker and a sob.

She touched his leg. "It's not quite three months, and you'll visit for five days in the middle. Right?"

He felt childish, standing with his arms crossed while she was the one who had to do everything hard—work long hours in a hospital all summer, leave the perfect weather of southern California, put up with him—and yet, he couldn't help himself. Who knew if she'd ever come back?

"Danny," she said, and she opened her arms as he fell into her.

———

THE SNOW WAS BLINDING on Heavenly Mountain, great streaks of white in varying hues. In the distance, the ski lift broke through the haze like a lifeline, thin, gray cables transporting the barest of vehicles, mere outlines against the white.

Jess waited for his wife near the resort exit. Mists of icy water coated his face, and he pulled his beanie down over his ears. The cap was reggae-colored—orange, green, black—and hand-crocheted by his daughter, Jenny, in camp the summer before.

What would they do next summer, he wondered, if they no longer lived all together? Would the kids visit him for two weeks at a time? Would they be able to afford the summer camp?

Mati pushed through the revolving glass door in her purple ski jacket, goggles dangling from her hand, brown hair pushed back from her face by the wind. The intensity of the weather surprised her, but it was a delighted surprise, and she smiled and leaned into the cold vapor.

What was he thinking? They *had* to work it out. He couldn't lose her, couldn't imagine one night in a place without her.

"Did you get your coffee?" she asked. She pulled puffy, white gloves from her pocket.

The coffee maker in their room had sputtered and died that morning, emitting a final blast of coffee-scented steam. "I stopped by the restaurant," he told her.

"Where do you want to go first?" Mati zipped her jacket up to her neck and with gloved fingers, awkwardly pulled the fur-lined hood over her hair. Her cheeks were pink from the cold, her lips and dark eyes glistening. She was beautiful, as beautiful as the day he'd met her at a crowded party on a rooftop in downtown Los Angeles. Both had started working at the law firm earlier that year but hadn't met until the holiday fete under the hazy stars; each clutched a wineglass and shivered in the night air.

Now, standing on the cold mountain, Jess felt a rush of affection and reached for her. His own gloved hands slipped over her shoulders as he tried to catch hold. He had caught her off guard, and she took a lunging step with her right foot to get her balance, stumbling, and as he tried to grab her elbow, her waist, anywhere to right her, he pushed her, accidentally and too roughly, and she fell to her knees on the damp snow.

"Goddamn it, Jess." Her face clouded with anger. "You're so clumsy."

He reached down and helped to right her. She pulled on his arm, looking away as she stood up.

"Since when am I clumsy?" he said. "Is that another fault I've missed?"

She rolled her eyes. "You just knocked me over, for no reason!"

"Oh, right, I wanted to push you into the snow."

"I'm going inside," she said. "I need to use the bathroom."

"Again?" he asked, somehow outside of himself as he said it. What he wanted to say was *Please, let's stop. I love you. You look beautiful.*

She pushed the revolving door so hard she had to wait for a few rotations to safely walk through.

They had argued the night before about the temperature of the heater in their room. Mati had been "sweltering," whereas Jess claimed he'd been the most comfortable he'd been in possibly any hotel room, at any point in his life, and that he couldn't see any reason to change the setting. They had argued over breakfast about him reading the paper while she had nothing to do but stare at the people around them, all of whom were having conversations "like normal people." The long drive to the resort had been interminable, between listening to Mati's folk music or her phone calls to the office, while he drove the whole time, angry to be driving the whole time but unable to let her drive for even a short while, for God-knows-what reason.

His mother was staying with the kids. It was Friday, Jess remembered. She would have to take them to school and back. For one year, both kids were at the same middle school, Ben in seventh grade and Jenny in eighth. Ben would have football practice from five to seven and Jenny had a free night. Her piano had been rescheduled to Saturday morning. These long weekends away were more difficult to schedule, now that the kids were older. When they were younger, he and Mati would often slip away for three or four days. The kids loved staying with Mati's parents in the valley, or at home with Jess's mom, who said it was easier to watch them there than at her small apartment.

It was a partnership at home, with both of them working and the coordination it took to get Jenny and Ben to their activities, lessons, and games. Mati kept a family calendar in the kitchen, marked up with weekly events and reminders.

Yesterday, on the mountain, they'd almost died. It was like something from a dream, and Jess had to force himself to think about it. They had arrived after lunch, hoping to have Thursday afternoon and part of Friday before the weekend crowd arrived. They'd dropped their suitcases in the room and had hurried to hit the slopes.

To their surprise, the mountain was teeming with skiers. Even so, they were both relaxed and happy to be in the open, frosty air, grinning as they sped down the first run, he in front and her some distance back. On their second run, Jess made it to the clearing at the bottom of the trail and turned back to watch for his wife. And the scene suddenly before him was like something from a cartoon, a rolling, rowdy cloud of white lumbered down the mountain, peppered here and there with bodies, with legs and skis and ski poles. Items of clothing—a glove, a hat—shot from the small avalanche as it gained speed and girth. Jess had only a series of moments; he dug his poles into the slushy ground and catapulted himself over a stacked embankment, landing at the base of a pine tree. He heard the avalanche pass overhead, a curious, almost-soft sound that eventually fizzled out. He felt a light, cold spray and heard someone yelling from the top of the slope. Unlatching his skis, he peered over the embankment. Three bodies lay scattered and motionless, some distance away. He strained his eyes for Mati's purple jacket. Struggling to crawl back onto the slope, he slipped again and again on the icy ground. His eyes stung; he had lost one glove, and his hand burned from the cold. Finally, he stood on shaky legs and began to walk towards the dark figures in the snow.

Then, through the charged air, he heard his name and turned back the other way to see Mati gliding effortlessly down the hill. She slid to a perfect, snow plough stop right next to him, her eyes gleaming, unaware of what had preceded her. Relief flooded through him, warm as water.

That night, they had dinner at the resort restaurant, shrimp for her and steak for him, and fortified themselves with a bottle of Zinfandel. They talked about the accident, which had claimed the life of one man, a father like Jess, vacationing like they were, and about the other victim, a teenager with two broken ribs and a dislocated shoulder. He'd be fine, they agreed. A tourist from Denmark had escaped without injury. It took about two hours for the shock to wear off, and they'd begun arguing about Jenny and whether she should take two honors classes in high school the following year or maybe just one to see how much she could handle (his idea), along with her piano and soccer. Mati thought he was underestimating their daughter's talents; Jess thought his wife was expecting the kids to have the same drive she had. Later, they bickered about the heater in the room, he counted from one to one hundred as she took an eternity in the bathroom, and they went to sleep in the separate double beds she thought he had reserved rather than a king to avoid being near her.

So when Mati rejoined her husband at the front of the resort on that second day of their getaway after he'd accidentally pushed her down, Jess kept his distance. They spent the day skiing on separate slopes. Mati wanted to take it easy after the drama the day before; Jess wanted to challenge himself. In the evening, they ordered room service, and he watched a movie on television while she read a mystery novel.

When the fire started, both were buried under identical mounds, the thick, down comforters of their respective double beds. The room was cold, colder than it had been the night before because Jess had lowered the thermostat, out of spite, and when the flames traversed the hallway and licked the door to their room, he sleepily thought perhaps she had turned the heat up after all. He had a few, half-formed thoughts about her stubbornness as he kicked the comforter off his legs and fell back asleep.

It was the worst tragedy in recent Tahoe history; in all, thirteen resort guests succumbed to the fire, which started in someone's room with a forgotten hookah and devoured an entire wing. Some guests broke windows and jumped to safety. One man alerted the travelers in at least a dozen rooms, garnering himself an interview on a local news station and a lifetime of gratis ski fees at Heavenly. Others, such as Jess and Mati, died, most likely from smoke inhalation, which social workers assured the victims' families was a fast and merciful way to go.

———

DANIEL LOOKED up at the class. Most eyes were pointed downward, but Alyssa gave him an encouraging half-smile.

Someone coughed, then coughed again. Then it turned to

what sounded, unbelievably, like a chuckle. All eyes moved to Brandon, who leaned over his desk. He took a sip from his Starbucks cup then coughed again. Only it wasn't exactly a cough, more like a stifled laugh.

"Which of you brave souls will start?" Mr. Brooks said.

A flash, something his mother used to sing: I have heard of a land on a faraway strand, tis a beautiful home of the soul.

Daniel scanned the room of faces, waiting.

Brandon wiggled in his seat, took another sip, and cleared his throat.

"Great detail," Alyssa said. "I really liked the interactions between them. It seemed to be a true representation of a struggling marriage. Believe me, I can relate!"

No one laughed.

A flash, his mother sitting on the back stoop after an argument with his father. You have more creativity in your little finger, Daniel, than I've ever had. It's a tool and a strength, remember that.

"I appreciate your effort with the rewrite," Dean said. "But just so I have this straight—you saved them from the avalanche so they could die in a fire caused by a hookah? I'm sorry, but I don't get the point of that. I think I preferred the avalanche."

A flash, his parents laughing about something on television. His mother's face buried in his father's chest, her hair falling all around, her shoulders shaking.

A smothered burst came from Brandon. His tee shirt was bunched up over his belly and his face was bright red. "I'm sorry," he said, squirming in his seat until he finally stood up. His chair scraped loudly against the floor, and they watched as he hurried from the room. As the door closed, they heard muffled coughing in the hall.

A flash, the back seat of a black car as they followed another, larger black car. Smeared windows, a mercilessly sunny day. The radio turned to local news.

Slowly, Daniel gathered his papers and trudged back to his desk.

———

IN HIS TEENAGE BEDROOM, a framed Nirvana poster hung over the bed. A baby, underwater and framed in blue, reaches for a dollar bill on a fishing line. His aunt never appreciated the poster, because the baby's privates were in full view, and yet she'd kept it on the wall for the three years he'd been in a dorm at UC Santa Cruz. When Daniel discovered the band as a teenager, the lead singer had already been dead for twenty years. His friends thought it very retro of him when he started listening to the grunge bands of the nineties, and they indulged his purchase of a turntable and LPs. Around this time, Aunt Mathilde had lugged two boxes of folk records into his room—his mother's collection—but Daniel had never taken the time to listen to any of them. The boxes were still stacked in his closet.

He went to the kitchen for breakfast, and as he hunched over a bowl of shredded wheat, he looked for a message from Jane. Nothing. He had called at eleven o'clock the night before, and again at twelve-fifteen. Now it was late morning, and she still hadn't answered. He sent her a text: "You up?"

She answered right away. "Yes, you?" Followed by a wink emoji.

It wasn't like her to be flirty via text. Was she overcompensating for something? He decided to call her.

She sounded groggy when she answered and he pictured her, half-dressed, amidst a mountain range of blankets and sheets. "Where are you?" she asked.

"Fremont," he said.

"Oh, good. I'm glad you went home for the weekend." She stretched, making little cat-like noises. "How is everyone there?"

"I think my aunt had her tennis group this morning. Uncle Leo's golfing."

"What a life," she said. "You and your country club."

"It's their country club."

"Yes, but you and Jessica are members too. Lucky."

He wanted to respond but didn't. Usually Jane was sensitive about the facts of his life, maybe even overly so. How anyone could think it "lucky" to lose your parents at age fourteen and go live with your aunt and uncle, no matter how well off they were, was beyond him. True, they were kind and gracious people, and they welcomed Jessica and him into their family without hesitation. True, he had enjoyed hanging out with his cousins, both boys around his age and yes, true, they had a country club membership and spent summers golfing and playing tennis and lounging by the clubhouse pool in their neighborhood. Maybe it was lucky after all, he thought, although it had never felt that way.

"How did it go last night?" he asked. "Did you end up working late?"

"Pretty late," she said. "All the interns went out for drinks after."

"Who?"

"Everyone. Lisa, Amal, Michiko, Gary, Aaron."

Aaron was the one he'd heard too many stories about. Aaron, the muscle-bound rower and lover of vintage cars. Aaron, the amazing, improvisational chef. Daniel listened while Jane talked about the exciting neighborhoods of Boston, her interesting fellow interns, and the stimulating work they were doing.

Aunt Mathilde came through the back door, wearing an orange tennis dress and holding a grocery bag. She was tall like his dad had been but lacked his dark, striking features. His other aunt, Lisa, had brown hair and eyes but wasn't particularly tall. Each had just enough resemblance to pluck a chord in Daniel.

"I should get going," he said to Jane. "I need to do a little work on that new story. This is the last week of class."

"He's having everyone rewrite something this time?"

"Yeah."

"Did you decide what to do?"

"No," he said. "Not really."

Aunt Mathilde started unpacking groceries.

"I'll call you later," he said.

"Okay," Jane said. "I should be home early tonight. Maybe text me first, because I've been turning off the sound, and then I forget and miss everything."

"I miss you," he said.

Her voice softened. "I know. Me too. It won't be—"

Too late, he realized he had cut her off. He looked over and his aunt was busily unloading things from her bags, pretending not to listen. "Did you get Cheerios?" he asked her.

"Sorry," she said. "I forgot. You found the shredded wheat, I see, and there's the granola Jessica likes."

"You got Jess's cereal and not mine?"

She patted his head on her way to a cupboard. "Poor Danny."

He stared out the window at the green expanse of the backyard. In the distance, a cobblestone path led to the community pool and clubhouse. Beyond that, an idyllic man-made lake was stocked with koi and ducks, and a white gazebo jutted out, where people took pictures for weddings, proms, and family reunions. Three miles away was the country club with its groomed links and mahogany-accented rooms. "Can I ask you a question?" he said.

"That sounds serious." She sat on the bar stool across from him and folded her hands on the polished granite island.

"Do you think I grieved for my parents in a normal way? I mean, do you think I'm repressed or avoiding it? Or the other extreme—do you think I'm fixated in some way?"

Her eyes narrowed. "I'm not sure anyone ever really gets over something like that. Speaking from my experience, I think about my brother every single day. Some days it's a dull pain but others, I forget time has passed, and it's fresh and sharp." She shook her head. "Where's this coming from?"

He shrugged. "Every story I write seems to include some terrible accident. I never thought about it, not really, but the professor pointed it out and asked me to try something different." He swirled his spoon around the milk remaining in his bowl. "I think maybe it's a theme I'm working through, you know, interrupted life."

She propped her chin on your hand. "I thought you were supposed to take from your experiences. Isn't that what they say, 'Write what you know?'"

"And that's why I don't think I'm writing about my parents at all. Because I don't really know anything."

"What do you mean? You know about the train trip to Napa and what happened."

"Yes, yes." He dropped his spoon into the bowl loudly. "But I don't know anything about them, not really. I know they took care of me and got me what I needed. I know my mom used to be a singer, until she had me and Jess and later, she started working as a secretary at the law firm. I know my dad was an accountant and he had recently gone back to school to get some degree. But the rest, what kind of people they were—"

Aunt Mathilde nodded. She reached up and smoothed a few stray strands away from her face. "You were a teenager when they died. It isn't until you get older, much older, that you begin to understand some things about your parents and begin to know them as people. I'm sorry you and Jessica won't get that opportunity. You can always ask me any questions you have about them."

Daniel leaned back, crossing his arms over his chest. "I'm not sure I was meant to be a writer."

"Have you ever tried to write about what happened?"

"According to my writing class, that's all I'm writing about."

She reached over and put her hand on his forearm. "I mean, write about what you remember, from start to finish, to get it out of your system."

"Maybe," he said.

She stood up and stretched.

He watched as she straightened up the kitchen. After that, he knew she'd take a shower, put on one of her long, patchwork skirts and start to think about what to make for lunch before his uncle got home. Then she'd water the plants on the back porch, fold some laundry, and bring in the mail. At some point, she would swoop in and make his bed without him seeing, like some bed-making ninja. She may pour herself a glass of iced tea and sit on the porch with a book. She liked mysteries and recently, they'd started talking about the authors she enjoyed. He knew she had grown up in the Bay Area with her two siblings, his father and their much-younger sister, Lisa, who lived in Idaho now; Mathilde rode horses as a girl until she broke her leg in a bad fall and their father forbade her to continue. Even now, she talked about horseback riding wistfully. She liked deep dish pizza and English comedies on cable. His aunt was the most efficient person he knew.

Daniel took his bowl over to the sink and stood for a moment looking out at the idyllic landscape. He thought about Jane and soothed himself. She'd either come back or she wouldn't and either way, he'd still be here. He couldn't bear thinking about the alternative.

He walked over and grabbed his backpack from a hook near

the back door. It was where his aunt hung her jackets and keys, and plastic bags filled with things that needed to go out or come in. Slinging it over his shoulder, he headed into his uncle's home office to work.

———

"HEY, LOSER." Jessica poked her head into the room.

"Hey," Daniel said.

She wore a dusty pink sweatshirt with Stanford written across the chest in big, block letters. Her hair was pulled back into a loose ponytail, but even from his position at their uncle's desk, he could see that it was the same, dark blonde that sparked red in the sun. This, and the way she carried herself, or maybe the smile teasing the corners of her mouth, this sudden, intense familiarity—something caused a pang deep within him.

"When did you get here?" she asked.

"Thursday," he said.

Jessica perched on the edge of the couch next to the desk and crossed her arms. There was always purposefulness about her, an intent. She'd been student body president in high school, popular and well-liked. At her graduation, Daniel had watched, along with his aunt and uncle, as she approached the podium time and again for awards. He'd always thought she'd be a lawyer or a teacher, someone who would thrive on convincing people about something. She was in her second year as a Public Policy major and although he wasn't entirely sure what that meant, Daniel knew his sister meant to change the world.

"Did you visit Grandma?" she asked now.

He shook his head. "Not this time."

"She's doing well." She pushed the sleeves of the sweatshirt up to her elbows. "Still doing her game night on Wednesdays and church stuff. I wish you'd go over there and get those base-ball cards. She brings it up every time I'm there."

"Hm," he said.

His sister's college was a quick thirty-minute drive home, while it could take him up to an hour-and-a-half from Santa Cruz, depending on traffic. This made Jessica's visits much more frequent, and she never failed to find a way to remind him of this fact.

"How did she end up with those cards, anyway?" she asked.

"I don't know."

"Well, you should get them, at least bring them over here." She brought one leg up and propped her ankle on her lap. "Have you been to any Giants games this year?"

He lifted his hands from the computer keyboard, where they'd been hovering since she walked in. "No, I've had this summer course." He still watched baseball, occasionally, and kept track of statistics online, as he'd done as a kid by poring over the sports section of the newspaper—now online. Once in a while, he thought about getting a ticket, asking Jane if she'd like to go. For some reason, he never did.

She leaned over and tried to get a look at the computer display. "What're you working on?"

"A story." He sat up straighter. "It's a writing class. How's the summer job?"

"You know," she said, shrugging. "Lots of filing." She looked towards the window, where a lone oak provided relief against the green span of lawn. "Do you want to go swimming in a while?"

"I didn't bring a suit," he said.

"Borrow one of Uncle Roy's." She raised her eyebrows, and they both chuckled. Their uncle was a tall, portly man with a fondness for bright patterns.

She stood up. "I'll let you get back to work then."

"Wait," he said. "Can I ask you something?"

"Sure."

"What do you remember, you know, about them?"

Quietly, she took a long breath and rested against the couch again. "It's funny you should bring that up. Today, when I was with Grandma, I had this thought, and I can't seem to shake it. When she came to stay with us, before we came here, do you remember how she cooked and cleaned and took care of everything? I mean, you were a wreck, and I was sort of numb, both of us stumbling around in our own worlds. She brought dinner to your room and didn't say a word about it."

He nodded, remembering.

"I was thinking," Jessica said, her eyes widening. "He was her *son*." She shook her head slightly. "We were having a tough time, sure, but can you imagine? And she came and helped, and never once did I think about what she must have been feeling."

Daniel closed his laptop with a loud snap.

"I remember you let me sleep in your room," she said. "You were barely speaking, but you let me come in and maybe that would seem weird to someone else—what were we, thirteen and fourteen? But it wasn't. I'll never forget that. It reminded me I wasn't alone."

He cleared his throat. "But you're talking about *after*," he said. "I guess what I meant was, and maybe it wasn't clear, but what do you remember from *before*?"

"Oh." Something flashed across her face. She stood up, pulled down the sleeves of her oversized sweatshirt. "Can we talk more later? I was hoping to get to the pool before dinner."

He glanced at the clock. It was one o'clock in the afternoon. "Okay," he said.

She walked towards the door, and there it was again, something in the straight but soft line of her shoulders, the unique tinge of her hair. At the door, she turned back. "See you later, loser." She tried for a mean smirk, but there was a kindness in her eyes.

Daniel scooted his chair towards the desk, opened his laptop, and waited for it to come back to life.

———

WHAT HAPPENED:

Daniel was playing tennis after school. He was a freshman and fought daily for his spot on the team, which was filled with boys who'd been playing for a decade or more. He'd picked up the sport two years before, after a week spent at his aunt and uncle's house in Fremont. They had a clubhouse where they lived, with a pool and tennis courts. When she saw his interest, his aunt bought him a racket, and his parents agreed to weekly lessons. He loved the pace of it, the intensity. He could escape during the game, forget about his failing math grade and the often-tense atmosphere at home. He felt competent and in control on the court. His life, at that point, was mostly about tennis.

His sister was a year younger, and he was glad to be in a different school, if only for a year. Jessica was outgoing and popular, loved school and socializing; she was his opposite in many ways. When they'd been in middle school together, she'd always make a big scene when she passed him in the hall, and her friends would giggle and call out his name.

He had just returned a difficult serve when he looked up and saw his grandmother talking to the coach. She'd been staying with them while their parents took a long weekend trip. They were going to look at some mansion and drink wine, which he thought sounded like a boring vacation. He wondered what his grandmother was doing there. Practice wasn't near being over; he had told her it ended at five.

The two adults walked towards him onto the court. His doubles partner let the ball sail past them, and all four players turned to watch. And it wasn't until they came closer that Daniel noticed the stricken look on his grandmother's face, her strained, wet eyes.

What he found out:

His parents had been on a wine-tasting train in Napa when the conductor, who had possibly been sampling wine himself, had somehow diverted the train onto the wrong track, on which an express passenger train was traveling in the opposite direction. His parents, who had splurged on first class seats to celebrate their sixteenth wedding anniversary, were among the thirteen people pronounced dead at the scene.

What he knew:

They had been fighting, off and on, for some time. He and Jessica had learned to turn up the radio or television when they argued. Usually, it was about money, or the state of the house, or about him and Jess and their failures (grades, messy rooms, attitude), or his mom's coworkers, who went out for drinks sometimes after work, especially one called Keith whom their dad believed was a "harasser." Also, his dad was unhappy with his job and stressed out with his additional classes, and he stomped and grumbled around the house most of the time. But sometimes, their parents could still be goofy and funny. Sometimes, his mom would sing one of her favorite songs—"Prairie Lullaby," "Bridge Over Troubled Water," "Both Sides Now," or something else—and his dad would stop what he was doing to listen. His dad liked baseball, especially the Giants, and at least twice a year, he'd take Daniel to a game. His dad was tall and strong and liked to cook breakfast on Sundays. His mom smelled good, all the time, like flowers and fresh clothes. Daniel didn't know them as much as he would have liked to, didn't appreciate them as much as he should have, didn't tell them or thank them or love them nearly enough. And everything stopped for them, with a stupid accident on a stupid train, during a stupid trip that in a strange way Daniel was glad they took, because it meant they still wanted to try, and love, and stay married. And he felt sure his mom, kindred soul that she was, would want him to write about it however goddamn much he wanted, for as long as he wanted, until he couldn't or didn't want to write about it anymore. And that is how this story ends, how it will always end. Two people were on the earth and then they weren't. Two kids had parents and then they didn't. Life interrupted, and then it went on.

ABOUT THE AUTHOR

Mary Vensel White is the author of the award-winning young adult novel *Things to See in Arizona*, and the novels *Bellflower, Starling,* and *The Qualities of Wood,* the first book published under the Authonomy imprint of HarperCollins. Her short fiction and essays have appeared in numerous publications. She is an English and writing professor, an editor and publisher, and the current president of the California Writers Club, Orange County branch.

Born in Los Angeles, Mary has lived in northern California, Denver, and Chicago, and now resides back in SoCal. She believes in second chances—in most cases—and in our ability to imagine and forge a new path.